WITHDRAWN

D1320629

j
c.5

Coatsworth, Elizabeth
   The golden horseshoe.   Rev. by the
author.   Illus. by Robert Lawson.
Macmillan [1968, c1935]
   153 p.   illus.

Children's Catalog

     Title

The Golden Horseshoe

SIC JUVAT TRANSCENDERE

MONTES.

At Stafford Green.

The Golden Horseshoe

ELIZABETH COATSWORTH

Revised by the author

Illustrated by Robert Lawson

J
c.5
Coatsworth

The Macmillan Company, New York
Collier-Macmillan Limited, London

DAVIS BRANCH
YOLO COUNTY LIBRARY
315 EAST 14TH STREET
DAVIS, CA 95616

FOR MY MOTHER

*To whom courage and gentleness
have always been as natural as
breathing.*

COPYRIGHT, 1935, BY THE MACMILLAN COMPANY
COPYRIGHT RENEWED 1963 BY ELIZABETH COATSWORTH BESTON

All rights reserved. No part of this book may be reproduced
or transmitted in any form or by any means, electronic or
mechanical, including photocopying, recording or by any
information storage and retrieval system, without permission
in writing from the Publisher.

The Macmillan Company, New York
Collier-Macmillan Canada, Ltd., Toronto, Ontario

Library of Congress catalog card number: 35-18415
Printed in the United States of America
Originally published 1935
Reissued with revisions by the author, 1968

CC 6-24-10 PHR

CONTENTS

The Golden Horseshoe

TAMAR'S BAPTISM

She was baptized at a font which the Indians
   Stole from the church before she was born,
And carried away to a far-distant village
   To use for grinding their Indian corn.

Water is sacred, and corn is sacred—
   Corn that grows swaddled in green and pale silk,
Amid its great leaves, the Indian treasure
   Of dark sweet kernels and dripping milk.

Squash and pumpkin, tobacco and sunflower,
   Each one is beautiful, born of our soil,
But corn is the scepter, corn is the power,
   The giver of life and rewarder of toil.

The font was returned to the church and the parson,
   And the small shadowed pool lay again within stone;
But they noticed that children baptized of its waters
   Were quiet of eye, strong of sinew and bone.

I

STAFFORD GREEN

BIRDS flew up from the lawns and down from the branches of the great tulip trees on the terrace. Beyond the last box-hedge flowed the wide expanse of the James reflecting the clouds on its pale copper surface. The breeze that stirred the dining-room curtains had the smell of roses and river water in it, a Negro gardener was singing, some guinea hens creaked sleepily in the shadow of a bush, and a horse neighed from the stables beyond the wing of the house.

To-day young Caesar, Roger Stafford's body servant, was helping Scipio, the butler, serve dinner since it was his master's thirteenth birthday and Roger was to dine with his father, Colonel Antony. The boy was full of the importance of the occasion. He rearranged a flower in the big bouquet in the silver bowl and stood off to observe the effect. He, too, was thirteen.

"Don't know how young Master's going to like Missy coming in for dinner, too, like she was nigh to grown-up. Missy's only eleven, and seems like somehow young Master likes better to be by himself."

Old Scipio shook his head.

" 'T'ain't Missy being young," he said, "that Master Roger don't like—" He stopped himself as though he had said too much and glanced uneasily at the two portraits which hung opposite one another on the paneled walls.

They were the portraits of Roger's mother and of Tamar's, both dead. But in the paintings the two seemed always young and alive. Each wore the same heavy pearl drops in her ears and the same thick necklace of pearls about her throat, but there the likeness ceased. Mistress Evelina Stafford, Roger's mother, was fair and smiling with yellow ringlets and a look of gay pride in her blue eyes. She had come of the great Whitely family, which had given a royal governor to the province and was noted for its courage and arrogance. Mistress Honor Stafford, Tamar's mother, who

4

had been called Shadow-of-Trees in the Indian language before her husband chose an English name for her, was dark and grave. The great pear-shaped pearls hung against a smooth brown cheek, and under the necklace the artist had painted the faint tattooing of a running deer. But she wore her curled wig and dress of stiff brocade as though she had been accustomed to them all her life, and her eyes had a look of quiet dignity, as proud in its own way as Mistress Evelina's careless glance.

Voices were heard in the hall, Colonel Antony's heavy booming tones, mingled with the lighter ones of the children.

"I am sorry, Roger," he was saying, "that Captain Hoskins and the *Merryweather* have been delayed. I commissioned the Captain to buy the finest saddle he could find in London for that strawberry colt of yours, and a pair of silver spurs. But wind and wave care little for birthdays, my lad, and you will have to wait, it seems."

Young Caesar, overhearing the conversation from his position by the sideboard, clapped his hands silently, as excited as his unseen master, whose voice answered:

"Thank you, sir, you'll have no need to be ashamed of Rambler, and I hope not of me."

Another voice, low and eager, chimed in—

"You may have my cosset lamb, Roger."

"Oh, thank you, Tammy, lambs are for girls," said Roger loftily.

Colonel Stafford burst into laughter, as he appeared in the wide door, a hand on the shoulder of each child.

"Hear the young cock clap his wings, Tamar!" he cried. "Keep your lamb, my little lady, and he shall have his pick of Diana's pups, instead. Here," he added, pointing to the chair on his right, "sit down, Roger, sit down. It is your birthday and we must drink your health."

Roger, about to sit down, looked up, and hesitated, his fair face flushing at what he saw.

"Please, sir," he said, "may I sit on your other side? Let Tamar have this place."

Colonel Antony, already seated, looked up in surprise, his bright blue eyes kindling under shaggy brows.

6

"What's wrong with that place, sir?" he demanded. "Why should Tamar have it?"

"Because, sir, it looks towards my mother," answered Tamar for Roger, her voice hot with anger.

Colonel Antony gazed from one child to the other, a quick glance at Tamar, straight-haired, brown, her head thrown high, her dark eyes bright with anger and tears; and then turned towards Roger, his only son, who faced him obstinate and disdainful.

"Well," he asked the boy, curtly, "what have you to say, sir?"

"I should rather look towards my own mother, sir," Roger answered with a certain dignity.

Colonel Antony's brows drew together in a frown.

"You will sit where you are placed, sir," he said. "And believe me, I shall permit no slights on the memory of my wife from anyone, least of all from my son. Your stepmother's dignity should be as dear to you as to Tamar. I wish you to recall that among her own people she was the daughter of a queen, of the same blood as Pocahontas who was honorably received at the royal court."

"An Indian queen," murmured Roger under his breath.

7

"Silence, sir!" thundered his father. "Or back you go to eat in the schoolhouse for the ill-mannered boy that you are. Tamar, my love," he added in a tone of real tenderness, "you are not eating. Come, forget your brother's boorishness. We will pledge together the two loveliest ladies who ever gathered roses in the gardens of the James."

Tamar, her lips to her goblet, looked quickly towards Roger, hoping that he might give her one of his bright, warm smiles; but he drank staring stonily in front of him. His masculine pride had been hurt by a reprimand before Scipio and young Caesar.

"A curse on these Indians," he thought to himself. "They spoil everything. Why need Father, one of the greatest gentlemen of the Dominion, have fallen in love with a savage and brought her back to take my mother's place?"

The echo of an old servant's laugh that he had heard long years ago was in his ears now: "Master's gone crazy-mad and wedded himself to an Injun lady out of the woods. It's enough to make Miss Evelina turn in her proud grave. I never heard tell of such goings-on in all my born days."

The words had rankled in Roger's heart all his life.

The words had rankled in Roger's heart all his life. Sensitive, upright, and full of the pride of race, for this act alone Roger criticized his father, who had mixed Indian blood with the blood of the Staffords.

Roger's memories of Madame Honor herself were vague: a light step, a low voice seldom used, a kind touch against which he had set his will—these were all he remembered. Yes—and of seeing her at the foot of the great stairs, in a white dress, holding a fan in her hand, receiving guests at his father's side; and once of going with her for some forgotten reason through a light rain at dusk, while she saw to the roosting of the hundreds of ducks and chickens and geese of her poultry-yard. The Negro boys drove the guinea fowl, uttering their creaking call, out of the box-hedges, and some young girls brought in a flock of turkeys from feeding in the woods. They guided them with switches, and the turkeys ran forward with stretched necks, gobbling. Madame Honor watched them, under the hood that shadowed her face.

"They are the Indian birds, little Roger. I love them best of all the things at Stafford Green," she had said.

Suddenly he realized that she had confided to him that day her unhappiness. In spite of jewels and fine dresses, she had been lonely in this great house of Stafford Green, waited on by many servants, entertaining his father's friends who came for visits in their great coaches, speaking a language not her own, and living all day by a tradition to which she had not been bred. She had never made a mistake. Her dignity had never faltered. But she must have longed for the cool green of the forest, for the rustle of the underbrush opening leafily as she passed through it, perhaps even for the little brass bells she had worn in the fringes of her girdle.

The boy had a natural sympathy, but here where it ran against his inherited pride he caught himself up angrily. Madame Honor had taken his mother's place, and had left him with a half-Indian sister, and that he must not forgive. It was all very well when they were with their cousins and Virginian friends who seemed to think little about it, but Governor Spotswood and his English-born secretary were coming soon. What would they think of Colonel Antony Stafford for having a daughter who was half a wild Indian?

Roger's face reddened with imagined shame, partly for himself and partly for this little sister of his. Why couldn't Tamar have been like the other boys' sisters? And he stared across at her with miserable eyes.

Tamar promptly stuck her tongue out at him, and then went on decorously spreading honey on hot bread.

II

ARRIVALS

LIFE on the plantations came and went by the river. It was the road to London and to all the world. Down the broad currents of the James were carried the great cargoes of tobacco from the plantations, the corn, the deer hides and beaver skins; between miles of forest where the grapevines hung from the topmost branches of the trees, and the deer looked up with dripping muzzles at the distant creak of cordage; past scattered plantations with their wharves and storehouses; past swamps where the rough-barked tapering cedars grew from black soil barely drained by crawling streams; past a few Indian villages of "long houses" covered with bark or rough mats, standing among scattered trees where grew the little gardens of corn and tobacco and squashes; down to the rounding sand-dunes where all day long the sea-birds screamed and the ducks rose in great flocks from the wild grasses growing in the estuaries, and where sometimes in spring the white swans lay like a flotilla of newly launched vessels—and so past the islands where the pirates lurked, and out to the buffeting sea.

And up the river came the rum and molasses and sugar from Jamaica, the slaves bought from the Dutch African traders, and all the luxuries from England that filled the great houses.

The children's eyes always wandered to the river. There was a Negro fishing, there came an Indian canoe, there a small boat rowed by slaves slowly fought the current, and they knew that one neighbor was about to visit another. The big vessels cast the reflections of their sails in the same waters. Once Colonel Antony had called the children to the windows to watch a fine ship go by. Later they had heard that it brought Governor Spotswood, who had with him a vast cageful of English larks to let loose in the meadows of Virginia. The poor birds had not lived, her father said, but Tamar liked the Governor for that fancy. She was glad that he was soon to come to Stafford Green.

One morning a servant hurried up with the news that the *Merryweather* with Captain Hoskins was beating up stream towards the landing. The children had an especial interest in her coming because their former tutor had returned to England and the agent was sending them another on this voyage. Roger, who was with his father when the news came, went in search of his sister. He found her at the kennels, which lay near the stables, forge, and carriage rooms, in separate buildings to the right of the house.

Tamar did not notice her brother's approach followed by young Caesar. She was sitting back on her heels, a little smile on her lips, absorbed by the scene before her. In the warm dust of the kennels lay a hound nursing a litter of fat half-grown puppies. But among the puppies, and taking up more than its share of room, was a lamb kneeling and nursing with the others, its long tail waggling. At sight of Roger, the dog raised her head and gave a thump or two with her tail.

"Lie still, Diana," said Tamar. "You're the only hound in the Dominion that has a lamb for foster-child."

But Roger at that moment had no eyes for dogs or cosset lambs.

"Tamar!" he shouted breathlessly, "the *Merryweather* is coming up river. She'll be tied at the wharf in half an hour. My saddle's in her, you know, and Mr. Reid, too."

Tamar rose to her feet in one smooth motion and brushed her skirts.

"Tell young Caesar to bid Agnes bring me a kerchief," she said. "I must have something to wave to Captain Hoskins as he comes in. Where is Father? Let me hold your hand, Roger. I wonder what manner of man Mr. Reid will be?"

Even the Colonel was at the wharf as Captain Hoskins brought his vessel alongside. But though the Colonel was nearly as curious as the children about his commissions, he first took the Captain to the great house to pledge his safe return and ask him the details of the voyage. With them went Mr. Reid, a tall young man with a long bony face and observant gray eyes.

"Mr. Reid will be given over to your entertainment

later," said the Colonel as he introduced him to the children. "Just now, he must be my guest."

Roger saw the stranger's eyes resting long on Tamar. "What is he thinking?" the boy asked himself. "Is he thinking she looks half a savage?"

But already Mr. Reid's back was turned and he was walking off with the other gentlemen.

The boy turned back with Tamar to watch the unloading. Beyond the sailors in their wide breeches and ragged white shirts was a group of four or five rather rough-looking men and a girl. Landsmen, they seemed wan and listless after the long voyage. Roger eyed them a moment, and guessed they were indentured servants come from England to work for a term of years as virtual slaves. The Colonel would never hire any on his estates, and Roger had inherited his dislike of the trade.

"Young Caesar," he said quickly, "run along up to the big house and bring down stout and cornbread for these folk here. Get Scipio to help you. Victuals that don't smell of salt water will taste mighty good to them, I reckon."

Tamar came up and squeezed his hand. "Bring some cherries, too, young Caesar," she added. "Did you see any pirates, Mr. Gillespie?" she asked the mate, whom she had known all her life.

"Two sail, Miss Tammy, off the islands," he answered, "but we were well north. We'd have fit if we'd had to, but the wind was with the *Merryweather* and we kept well out of their way."

"I'm glad, Mr. Gillespie," said Tamar.

A horse neighed from the hold and instantly Roger was all interest. Mr. Gillespie, following his glance, nodded, "Yes, Master Roger, as pretty a piece of horseflesh as you'd wish to see, sir; a three-year-old named Grenadier we're bringing out for Mr. Nathaniel Bridge, who is secretary to the Governor."

"Then you can disembark him here, Mr. Gillespie, and let him get his land-legs, for the Governor is coming to Stafford Green next week," exclaimed Roger.

Tamar pulled his coat.

"That must be Father's new periwig," she said, pointing to a box. "And look, Roger! I do believe that's a spinet. I wonder if they have my striped dress with the hooped skirt, and the pills for old Nancy?"

There was a pounding of hoofs, and two sailors led a fine black horse to the gangplank. He put one foot on the unsteady boards and snorted and drew back.

The two men attempted to force him forward by jerking on the halter, while a third sailor struck him on the flank.

"Here!" cried Roger with his father's air of authority. "That's no way to handle a horse."

He was stripping off his coat, when one of the indentured servants, who had been standing a little away from the others, stepped forward, his own ragged coat in his hands.

"Use my coat, friend," he said. "Thine would come to needless harm."

Roger nodded his thanks as he bound the garment over Grenadier's eyes, and stood beside the animal for a moment soothing him with voice and hand.

"Now, boy," he said, encouragingly, "up! You'll be on solid land in a moment."

A tug at the halter, a hollow rumble of hoofs, and Grenadier was out of the vessel, sniffing the air of a new continent.

Roger stood looking at him admiringly.

"A fine-looking beast," he said meditatively to the mate. "I wonder now how he would compare with my Rambler?"

"Begging your pardon, sir," said Mr. Gillespie,

"I'd trust the English-born horse against the Virginian."

"Then you'd put your trust in the wrong place," said Roger. "I'd wager, sir, a hundred pounds of tobacco to fifty that Rambler can show this horse his heels in a quarter-mile straight-away."

The mate laughed. "You can bet with Mr. Bridge, Master Roger," he said. "I'm not a gentleman and have no right by law to lay a racing wager," and he turned back to overseeing the work.

Meantime, Tamar had taken the coat and approached the man who had lent it. He was a little older than the other indentured servants, an ugly-enough smallish man with beautiful eyes.

"Thank you kindly," she said, a little shyly.

"It is thee who deserves thanks," he answered. "Thy cherries have renewed in me my trust in the Lord's kindness."

Tamar, about to turn away, paused and spoke gravely.

"Who are you?" she asked. "Why are you——" She hesitated.

"An indentured servant?" he asked, smiling at her. "I am one of those they call Quakers, and life is not made very easy for us in England. I hoped that if I could come under a new sky I might find more peace there. In the world I am John Dummer, a weaver by trade."

"Good fortune go with you, then, John Dummer," said Tamar, looking at him thoughtfully.

She returned to Roger's side like a shadow and watched with him the parcels and crates put ashore, speculating on each. But she was quieter than usual, and when her father with the others came down the walk she ran to meet him.

"Father," she said, "there is something on the *Merryweather* I want with all my heart."

It was rare for Tamar to ask any favor. Her father looked at her with surprise.

"What is it, Tammy? Something for yourself?" he said.

The shadow of a smile crossed her lips and was gone.

"Yes," she said. "Father, there is a weaver there, a Quaker, among the indentured servants. He is not like the others. He might find a bad master. I want you to take him."

The Captain brought up John Dummer.

"But you know, miss, I never have indentured serv-ants," said her father.

Tamar looked serenely into his eyes.

"You will have this one to please me, sir," she said.

"Egad, then, let me have a look at the fellow," cried the Colonel. "If I don't like the look of him, I'll hear no more of the matter."

The Captain brought up John Dummer, and the two men stood for a moment looking at each other—a curious contrast: the great land-owner in his long coat of fine broadcloth laced with gold, his face hand-some and assured among the curls of his wig that flowed to his shoulders, a three-cornered hat on his head and a gold-topped cane in his hand, facing the ugly little crop-headed weaver, who looked back at him serenely.

"Why don't you doff your hat, sir?" demanded the Colonel, at last.

"We only doff our hats to our Maker, not to any fellow-creature," said the man quietly.

"Then, sir—" began the Colonel angrily, but Tamar slipped a cool hand into his.

"I want him to weave me a blue dress, Father," she said.

Her father looked down at her. "Pocahontas said she wanted John Smith to make copper bells for her. It is always the same story. But I will not be harder than Powhatan in his day. Have your weaver, my dear, and may your heart always be as tender." Then he looked up and frowned at the Captain. "Let me see the man's papers," he said gruffly. The Captain returned with them. Colonel Antony read slowly through the articles of indenture, then—

"Add that to my account," he said, tearing up the papers and letting the scraps fly. He turned to John Dummer. "You are a free man, now, and may go or stay as you will. I hope you will stay."

The other man looked at him, his mouth working a little.

"Thee is a fit father to thy daughter, friend," he said when he could speak.

"I like your compliment, sir," said Colonel Antony with a laugh. "Are you content, Tammy? I told you I would have no indentures here."

III

A QUEEN'S CROWN

THE next day began with a thunderstorm. First came the thunderheads, domed and golden; then the sky darkened and the tulip trees and the great water-oaks rustled with a sound like fear, and the lawns turned a curious, almost metallic green, and the lightning came in blinding sheets, still far off.

The children were in the schoolhouse with Mr. Reid. He had been glancing over their books and had reached for a worn copy of Horace.

"Listen," he said. "Here is a poem about woods such as yours," and he began to read the rich vibrating verses in Latin. Roger could follow the meaning, but Tamar caught only a word here and there. It was the music of the sound she loved, like wind in the pines or water against rocks.

A flash of lightning seared the room, and Mr. Reid put down the book, and went to the window.

"A storm is more awesome and more beautiful than any words written by a man, even Horace himself," he said. "We have no such tempests in my land."

Tamar had been waiting for him to finish his reading, as she did not like to interrupt.

"Pray, sir," she said, "may I fetch the cosset lamb? He will be frightened at the storm." And at his nod she darted down the rose-bordered path that led to the great house. In no time she was back, carrying the big lamb with some difficulty. Just as she reached the door, the storm broke, in a sudden onslaught of wind and great drops of rain splashing down on the dry earth.

Tamar caressed the lamb and let him go.

"He likes to be near us," she said, "in a storm, sir."

"Rambler is nervous, too," said Roger. "One of the stable boys goes into his stall to keep him quiet. But he's not afeared if Gray Whiskers is in his manger. That's the big tomcat you see about the stables, sir, and Rambler sets great store by him."

The conversation was interrupted by constant, almost simultaneous stabs of light that shone even through closed eyelids, and by thunder that vibrated in the foundations of the schoolhouse. For a few minutes they seemed the center of all the storm's fury; then longer and longer pauses began to come between the lightning and the thunder, and they knew that the storm had gone over.

"Beautiful as is your land," said Mr. Reid, "it is in your skies that you excel the Old World. But what do the red Indians do in such weather as this?"

"There aren't many Indians hereabouts any more, sir. Most of them have gone beyond the mountains," said Roger quickly, frowning at Tamar to say nothing.

She saw the frown but ignored it.

"There are some Weyanokes still, sir," she said tranquilly. "My mother's people. They live on a branch farther up the river."

Mr. Reid gave Tamar a pleasant look.

"Why, Tamar," he exclaimed, "then you are a real daughter of this lovely land, half forest and half rich mansions."

"He is taking it well," thought Roger with relief.

"Should you like to see my grandmother's crown?"

asked Tamar a little shyly. It was to her a great treasure and she rarely spoke of it.

"So your grandmother was a queen?" asked Mr. Reid. "Some day you must show it to me."

"I'll fetch it now, sir—" and, catching up her

hooded cloak from its nail beside the door, she was off, moving swiftly without effort through the shower.

In a few minutes she was back again, and without a word placed the crown in his hands. Mr. Reid handled it with care. It was a gilt coronet set with large red and green jewels of glass and paste, such as he had seen worn by actors. It seemed to him pretty and touching.

As though he were reading the tutor's thoughts, Roger said:

"It is all false, sir, as false as the peace the Governor made with the tribes. There was a great council in Williamsburg where the college is now, and the royal Governor gave a crown to each of the kings and queens. But that didn't keep him from taking their lands. There is scarcely enough game for the few that are left. And they trusted us. Had we not given their chiefs crowns?"

Roger spoke with a bitterness that surprised the tutor in one who obviously had not a drop of savage blood in him. Later he came to realize that, although the boy's pride was so sensitive that he suffered keenly from it, he had a feeling for justice that carried him beyond all prejudices when it was roused.

Tamar quietly took back the crown.

"My mother's mother did not know it was false," she said. "She loved it as much as though it had been real. She wore it at council meetings, sir. She was a friend to the English. She sent my mother to Williamsburg to be educated in the ways of the English, and it was there that Father saw her. She was very lovely to look at, and wise and sweet. I am as proud of her as of Father himself."

She looked with a sort of challenge at her brother.

"If I were a little savage, I should not keep boasting of it," he retorted sharply.

"I'd rather be an Indian than be a nose-in-the-air Whitely," Tamar taunted, and went on, in a sing-song chant:

"When Adam and Eve worked with spindle and spade
The Whitelys were fanning themselves in the shade!"

"Be still!" said Roger, turning white.

Tamar's look changed. She put the crown down and ran over to Roger.

"Truly, brother," she said, in a low voice, "I am sorry. I did not mean to hurt you, but you often hurt me, you know, and I forget to be kind."

"The fault was mine, Tammy," said Roger after a moment. "We will say no more about it."

Mr. Reid had taken no part in the conversation, believing that until he knew more about the children in his charge he might do more harm than good by

Mr. Reid handled it with care.

checking them before they had reached their own agreement.

Now he stepped forward. "Give me the crown, Tamar," he said. "I will put it safe here on the shelf over my head. And now let us take this atlas, here, and I will ask you a few questions."

That afternoon the sun came out and the whole garden and woodlands and the broad fields of tobacco shone and sparkled with dewdrops. A sound of singing rose from the quarters with the thin columns of smoke that marked the position of the cabins of the field-hands out of sight of the big house. Roger took Mr. Reid for a sail on the river which, too, seemed sparkling with the rain, but Tamar went with Mrs. Macdonald the housekeeper through store-rooms, kitchens, and bake-houses, the linen rooms and the poultry-yards, learning her duties in preparation for the day when she would be old enough to take charge of Stafford Green.

In the "simple room" they packed a small basket of medicines for the Negroes who were sick, including the pills that had come yesterday for old Nancy who had been Colonel Antony's nurse. Tamar went from cabin to cabin giving the medicines with her own hand, while Mrs. Macdonald advised the patients as to how to use them. The babies were all playing on the ground together, in charge of an old woman with a bright cloth outlining a small, serene face. Tamar had brought part of a cone of sugar for them and broke it between two stones, dividing the bits impartially among the small eager palms reached to her. The last piece she popped into the mouth of a child too small to come for it, and she and the housekeeper walked away while the children chorused like a pondful of frogs, "Thank you, Missy—Thank you, Miss Tammy."

Tamar loved the sound of the spinning wheels in the spinning house where four or five young girls were working, singing low together to the sound of the spinning. But she hurried on while Mrs. Macdonald was examining the work, and soon came to the house, with a rose growing over its door, where the weavers had their looms.

It happened when she entered that only one loom was being used, the one near the window overlooking the land sloping to the river. Tamar saw in a minute

36

that it was occupied by John Dummer. His ugly face lighted as he saw her. He took her outside to show her the great hank of woolen thread he had dyed that morning.

"But such a blue as it is, John Dummer!" she exclaimed with delight.

"It is for thy dress, friend," he said. "Not that one must set store in worldly pomps, but thee has a heart not tarnished by such things."

That evening Captain Hoskins supped again at Stafford Green. He told them of the plays he had seen at Drury Lane playhouse in London, and of the great court beauty he had met walking in St. James' Park, with soldiers of the guard marching ahead of her to keep the crowd from pressing in upon her too close to stare at her beauty. And in London everyone was dancing the Roger de Coverley, a gay romp and frolicking dance, said the Captain.

"I'll send a boy for my fiddle," added he, "and if you please, Mr. Gillespie shall come with his flute. And perhaps the young people will favor us with a minuet."

Monsieur Herriot, the itinerant dancing master,

37

had spent three weeks that spring at the plantation, so the children had learned the most fashionable steps. Bowing and curtseying, with fingers touching and parting, they went through the graceful motions of the dance, while the candles in their silver sconces and candelabra shone on Roger's smile and Tamar's grave intentness. Some day she would be a young lady, dancing with her admirers. Some day she would have a great house to keep like Stafford Green. Some day—

The gentlemen were applauding. The dance was over. Now Mr. Reid was called upon for a recitation. Tamar slipped to a chair by the open window. A smell of wet earth and leaves came to her nostrils. Outside, the stars shone bright in the sky, less flickering than the candles. They were shining down on Indian camp-fires, she thought, where her mother's people sat quietly talking over low flames, with the darkness about their shoulders like a blanket.

Sitting between candle-lighted room and star-lighted night, a wave of inherited longing seized Tamar for a life she had never known.

IV

THE GOVERNOR CALLS

THE day of Governor Spotswood's arrival was hot and damp and breathless. The bees hung heavy in the bending flowers, and the James flowed like liquid copper below the lawns with no breeze to ruffle the almost unendurable brightness of its waters.

Everyone had been up since daylight making preparations, for no one knew how many gentlemen would come with the Governor, and then there would be servants and grooms to be looked out for. Mrs. Macdonald had aired sheets and superintended the making of beds in the great guest chambers; from the kitchens came the smell of baking breads and cakes and the shrill directions of the cook; the stablemen were busy preparing the stalls for the guests' horses. Colonel Antony and Roger visited the cellars to choose the wines that were to be served. Tamar's share in the preparations was the cutting and arranging of the flowers.

She had never been very fond of gardens, and flowers in vases always seemed to her dying. These English blossoms that had to be tended and cared for so carefully and which bloomed each in its place had never touched her heart, but she loved the unexpected violets along the ditches, and the pale bright pink of the wild roses, and the honeysuckle that clambered over bushes and fences and hung even from the trees in bowers of fragrance where the spring birds sat singing. She loved the small gay sunflowers the Indians grew, and the water-lilies in the ponds—every flower that sprang hardy and sweet from the Virginia soil in its season. These Tamar looked at with delight, keenly aware of their fragrance; but it would never have occurred to her to take them from the places where they grew. They lay like light upon this wide land of peaceful rivers and great forests walling in the plantations which lay within their folds. But the English garden flowers were grown for display, and she knew that other people liked a house to be filled with them.

By the time she had cut enough for all the rooms, her thumb felt ready to drop off and she hated the flowers Agnes had carried into the shade on heaped-up wicker trays. But in the coolness of the pantries, as she arranged them in silver and crystal bowls, her thoughts had leisure to turn to the guests. Governor Spotswood had been born in Tangier. Roger and she had looked it up in the atlas, and Mr. Reid had told them about the North African pirates and Christian slaves, orange trees, veiled women, and towns surrounded by white walls. The Governor had been aide-de-camp to the great Duke of Marlborough and had fought with distinguished courage at Blenheim. Her father said he was a handsome merry gentleman. She hoped his secretary, Mr. Bridge, of whom no one had much to say, would be pleased with Grenadier, who was now completely recovered from the effects of his long voyage.

Agnes was calling her.

"Missy, Missy! Master, he says you put on your fine dress directly. Gentlemen come along soon."

Tamar, who had been dawdling, crammed all the flowers she had left into a single bowl and glanced at the effect. It seemed to her to look better than any of the others.

"Here, Juno," she said to one of the house girls, "put that on the spinet and see that none of the water spills," and she was off up the broad stair like a swallow.

The Colonel had on a suit of fine dark mulberry color with holland lace at the throat and wrists and silver buckles catching the light at knee and instep. Roger was in sky-blue that made his eyes seem to shine in his face. But Tamar chose a fawn-colored dress of heavy silk and wore no ornament but a string of small pearls. Looking at her, the Colonel was about to suggest that she might wear one of her gayer dresses and then he realized that nothing else would become her so well.

The Governor, accompanied by half a dozen gentlemen, rode up the drive in a cloud of red dust. Tamar picked him out immediately by his soldierly bearing and air of authority. Young Caesar ran down to hold his horse. In a moment Colonel Antony was clasping him by the hand.

"Sir, this is my son, Roger, and already your loyal

The Governor rode up the drive.

adherent, and my little daughter, Tamar, who must do you the honors of the house."

Roger bowed low and Tamar curtseyed.

"Welcome to Stafford Green, sir," she said formally, adding, "and will you tell us about Blenheim and how you were wounded and what the great duke was like?"

"You know the way to a man's heart already, Miss Tamar," said the Governor, smiling. "Bid a soldier tell you of his campaigns and he will love you for it."

Tamar smiled.

"Any way to your lordship's heart is well taken," said her father for her. "Come, sir, Scipio will bring you something cooling after your hot ride."

By this time all the gentlemen were dismounted and her father was welcoming each—Mr. Bridge, the Governor's secretary, and six or seven neighboring gentlemen at whose houses the Governor had stayed, and who had decided to ride on with him in the cordial Virginian fashion, where no invitations were necessary between house and house.

Several of the gentlemen were cousins of the Colonel's. There were family questions to ask and answer.

and much laughter and talk. Her father had trusted Tamar with assigning each guest to his chamber. Feeling sorry for Mr. Joseph Bentley, who stuttered and—as she knew—lived on a poor plantation of only five hundred acres, she gave him the rose chamber, which next to the Governor's was the finest in the house. Her father pinched her cheek and smiled as the guests followed the house servants to their rooms, followed by their own servants carrying their portmanteaux.

"It is lucky you are not at court, miss," he said affectionately. "Here, kindness is no crime, egad."

All the Governor's visit was a frolic. Tamar supped in the schoolroom with Mr. Reid, but from the open windows of the dining-room came the sound of laughter and singing and the calling of toasts. Colonel Antony had sent to Martin's Folly, the Jennings place, for two tumblers and a tight-rope walker who, he had heard, were passing from plantation to plantation. As darkness came on, the servants lighted many-colored lanterns hanging from the tulip trees on the terrace, where they looked like softly shining fruit. Colonel Antony had set grooms holding pine-knots lighted in the Indian fashion, on either side of the space where the mountebanks performed. The good smell of resin pleased Tamar's nostrils where she stood with her maid Agnes, hidden from sight in an opening in the box-hedge. The coolness of evening after a hot day flowed about her.

The men were tossing many bright balls in the air, catching and tossing them again; they were standing on one another's shoulders. She watched their hands lightly balancing against the darkness. The tight-rope walker moved among the lanterns, his feet sliding along the torch-lighted rope that seemed to Tamar so high.

"Agnes," she whispered, "go fetch John Dummer. Tell him I wish him to come."

So Tamar—between John Dummer and the deeply breathing Agnes who kept exclaiming, "Lord-a-mercy, Missy, that gentleman will sure wake up in Kingdom Come!" at the most exciting moments—watched the performance, which was partly hidden from them by the bodies of the grooms holding the pine-knots. It seemed all the more exciting, glimpsed in snatches. Tamar had seen the men, that afternoon,

47

hard-faced and bold-eyed with a whining impertinence in their manner. But that was by day. By night they became magical with the litheness and gayety of creatures from another world. All too soon the tight-rope walker had finished his supreme act, carrying a companion on either shoulder. High in the darkness they stretched out their arms and bowed deeply to the royal Governor, then leaped nimbly to the ground. The performance was over amid applause and cries of bravo! from the gentlemen. The Governor led off by throwing a handful of coins to the men, and the other gentlemen followed his example amid laughter and banter.

The pine-knot torches were extinguished. Breaking into groups, the gentlemen strolled on the terrace under the lanterns. It was time for Tamar to go.

"Did you enjoy the tumblers, John Dummer?" she asked.

"At first, Tamar," he said seriously, "I was troubled at seeing them, thinking it frivolity and worldliness to watch their handsprings and cavortings, yet not wishing to leave when thee had invited me. And then I thought that it was no harm to regard a lamb

48

romping in a field and that it was God who had given these young men their agility. And after that I humbled myself in my proud judgment and delighted as much as thee, thyself, in the work of the Creator as manifested in these young men."

"I am glad," said Tamar who did not altogether understand the Quaker's words, but knew that he was happy. "Good-night, John Dummer." And she slipped away into the house, climbing the stair followed by Agnes, carrying a candlestick.

Tamar's bed had once been sent as a gift to Powhatan from James the First, the English king, who hoped to make an alliance with the Indians. It had been set up under the trees by the river, and rough sailors had carefully tucked its fine sheets in place and pulled the quilts smooth. The Indians had feared at first that it might be some sort of trap in which to catch their ruler, but Powhatan had come to be very proud of it. The wood of the posts was a little blistered and streaked where rain had fallen on it, soaking through the roofs of bark and matting under which it had stood, and the embroidered hangings of crewel-work had at some time been torn and were

49

mended with feathers of red-birds and humming-birds. Her mother's kin had given it to Shadow-of-Trees when she went to live at Stafford Green, and Tamar had inherited it. Lying in such a bed it was not strange that Tamar dreamed that night not of candles but of pine-knots held in the hands of Indians in the great lodge of her ancestor Powhatan, and that the figures she saw dancing about the fire were sometimes those of the tumblers in their pied garments, and sometimes of warriors she had never seen.

V

A FOX-HUNTING LAMB

THE next day was cooler. Clouds chased across the blue sky like a pack of hounds pursuing the sun, which seemed to shake them off with a brandish of golden antlers. The scene was doubled in the mirror of the James and silent shadows raced over the lawns. Even the trees tossed their crests lightly like horses impatient of the rein.

"Come, this day was made for hunting," said the Governor after the gentlemen had breakfasted late and merrily. "Have you foxes, Colonel Antony? I know you have hounds."

"My foxes are as good as my hounds and sometimes better," laughed the Colonel. "Gentlemen, what say you to a day of sport?"

"We'll see what Grenadier says to Virginian hunting," exclaimed Mr. Bridge, who was very well pleased by the look of his new horse and inclined to boast. "I should not be surprised, gentlemen, if he taught the native horses something on their own ground."

"I—" began Roger, and stopped; he had meant to retort, but remembered in time that Mr. Bridge was a guest under his father's roof and checked himself. Of all the party, the secretary alone struck a jangling note, and even the Governor spoke to him with a formal courtesy, noticeably different from his usual careless friendliness. Mr. Bridge was no choice of his, but some great lord's son who had a bad reputation in London at the card-tables and had been sent out to Virginia by His Majesty's government to oblige the family. He was an overbearing young man with a hanging underlip and a petulant expression, always saying how poor Virginian things were as compared with British, and talking about "natives" and "provincials" until the great land-owners stiffened at his insolence. He had, too, the persistence of a horse-fly, and having seen Roger's quick flush of annoyance, it was like him—when the gentlemen had mounted— to draw his black Grenadier over beside Rambler and say, smiling his insolent smile, as he tapped his boot with his riding crop, "I take it, my boy, our horses are of an age and weight, but I think mine will be nearer the fox."

"Perhaps, sir," said Roger, inwardly determined to outride the secretary if he had to break his neck to do it. He was looking forward to the day, a great one in his life, since it was the first time he had been allowed to ride in an official hunt. Not a horse there, not even the Governor's, was so clean-cut and fine-looking as Rambler, he thought, except perhaps Grenadier, much too fine a horse to belong to his new master.

Any further conversation was interrupted by the entrance of the hounds, the horns were sounded, and the hunt was off.

Tamar waved to them from the porch, and everyone turned in his saddle to wave back to her, a small straight figure in a green dress against the old-rose brick of the house. If the great house with its wings of outbuildings all centering in the solitary child made a very pretty sight—and several thought it did —Tamar, too, was aware of the beauty of the scene before her, the gay colors of the men, the dainty gait of the horses, the flow of the pack, all under the bright changing sky.

"A girl never does as she wishes," she thought. But she was humming as she made her way towards the schoolhouse where she was to do sums with Mr. Reid. She was weak in sums. "Dull things they are, sir," she said to the tutor.

"But you will be a great lady, Tamar," he told her. "You must know enough of these dull things to manage your house wisely."

She liked the brick school-building with its white door and small-paned windows open to the breeze, bare and cool inside; Mr. Reid's bed was neatly made up in the corner, with a chest of drawers beside it. Mr. Reid was a shy man. Only with the children was he at his ease, but he had fallen in love with Virginia. Already he had begun a long ode in Latin to the beauty of its skies and wide rivers, the darkness of its pines, and the expanses of its fields where grew the barbaric tobacco, wealth of Indian kings.

The children accepted him and it was with a light step that Tamar made her way towards his quarters, stopping only to whistle at a redbird perched on a branch beside the path.

Meantime, the hunt rode on at a slow trot. Suddenly Governor Spotswood threw back his handsome head and burst into hearty laughter.

"What is that with the hounds?" he asked, touching his host's arm.

Everyone looked to see a large lamb trotting among the dogs.

"Egad, it's Tamar's cosset!" cried the Colonel. "Its mother deserted it, sir, and Tamar coaxed old Diana to feed it with her pups. Bless me, if now it doesn't think itself a hound."

All unconcerned by the gentlemen's shouts of

laughter, the lamb trotted on at its foster-mother's side.

"Ah, this is a wonderful land of ours," said the Governor, "where the lambs hunt foxes!"

"Egad, I'm afraid all this is very irregular," answered Colonel Antony with pretended seriousness. "Roger, see if you can call your sister's pet."

The gentlemen reined in their horses, the hounds stood lolling their tongues, and Roger called and called to the lamb, which paid not the slightest attention to him.

Then the whip in charge of the hounds tried by a few dexterous cuts of the lash to separate the lamb from the dogs; but the lamb, protected by his heavy wool, only gave a slight skip of surprise and burrowed his way deeper into the thick of the pack.

"He'll soon enough drop back when the run begins," said one gentleman. "Wait until the hounds catch the scent."

But when the pack was off, baying amid the cries of the hunters, the lamb tore, bounding, in their midst. Roger rode to one side of Mr. Bridge, taking his measure. He had to admit the man rode well, and his admiration for Grenadier increased as he saw him at work. The English horse rushed his jumps with more dash than Rambler, but perhaps not quite with Rambler's catlike dexterity. Altogether, he gave an effect of great reserve strength and few nerves.

Rambler, sensing that the other horse was his rival, kept trying to get his head, but Roger held him back. "All in good time," he thought. "Your turn will come, Rambler." And he nursed his horse's strength.

Mr. Bridge turned once or twice to grin at the boy and, although Roger forced himself to smile back, he felt that there was more of taunt than of friendliness in the Englishman's smile.

But just as the hunt was stringing out, and horses and riders were showing their real mettle, and Roger was thinking the time had come to outride Mr. Bridge if Rambler could do it, he heard the Englishman curse ahead of him. Mr. Bridge had just jumped the trunk of a fallen tree, and Roger had only time to swerve Rambler as he followed, almost landing on the cosset lamb which stood bleating with exhaustion and panic. Grenadier was off at his strong canter with Rambler mad to follow, but Roger held his horse back. He was ready to cry from disappointment and vexation. This was the hunt to which he had looked forward so eagerly, and he had tacitly accepted Mr. Bridge's challenge. All his blood yearned to give Rambler his head, but he could not leave Tamar's lamb to be trampled. Mr. Bridge turned in his saddle to give him a derisive wave of the hand. Roger bit his lip to keep it steady.

"You little fool," he said angrily to the lamb. But he was not rough with it during the difficult task of getting back into the saddle of an excited horse while holding a large struggling lamb under one arm. At last he had it hoisted before him and turned Rambler homeward.

He had made his decision and did not regret it, but he had no desire to meet any of the hunt, with this humiliating burden. He turned Rambler to a path he knew through the pines. Where the forest touched the open the trees were festooned in a curtain of trumpet-vines, honeysuckle, and wild grapes whose leaves had turned their downy pale sides to the wind, forming an almost impenetrable barrier. Roger had to lower his head almost to Rambler's neck as

The path opened into a clearing.

they entered the straight wall of the woods, but—
once within—it was like coming into a great dark
room. The bright changing sunshine of the fields was
subdued here to long shafts of pale light in which the
floating spider-webs glistened. Little underbrush
grew among the old ridged trunks, but there were
patches of ferns and mosses, and the damp smell of
mushrooms and fungi mixing with the fragrance of
dry needles. A blue jay flew noisily down the arcade
of trees, a squirrel scolded. Speaking now to the horse,
now to the lamb, he succeeded in quieting them both,
and his own racing heart quieted with them. The trees
rose about him in endless rough pillars. The needled
branches swayed a little in the wind. The clamor of
horns and pack sounded faint and sweet in his ears.
To his own surprise the boy felt a sense of adventure
come over him, greater than when he had been riding
with the royal Governor and the other gentlemen.

The path opened into a clearing, sometimes used
for tobacco, but this year lying fallow. Roger saw a
herd of deer at the far end, grazing. They were to
the windward of him, so he pulled in Rambler to
watch them. In a moment he saw that there was some-

thing peculiar about two of the deer that appeared to be grazing at some distance from the others, but kept approaching them imperceptibly. He knew enough of Indian methods to guess that these two were hunters, each covered with a deer's hide, the antlered head stuffed with grass; and even as he watched he saw the climax of the hunt. The herd, grown suspicious at last, wheeled towards the forest, the hunters leaped upright, drawing their bows. He saw two arrows fly and a young stag fell, to be quickly killed by the knives of the Indians.

"I wonder who they are?" Roger thought, riding on. "Weyanokes, probably."

The tribes rarely came so close as this to the plantation, though occasionally a chief stopped to visit Colonel Antony. Roger would have ridden over to speak with the men, but the lamb in his arms impeded him.

He rode back to Stafford Green.

"Here is your cosset," he said to Tamar as she ran up.

"Oh, I am so sorry, Roger," Tamar exclaimed, wide-eyed. "I should have taken better care. He's spoiled the hunt for you."

"It is no matter," said Roger, touched by her sympathy. "There will be many other hunts, but there's only one fox-hunting lamb. The Governor was delighted."

VI

RUNAWAY

It was not long before Roger learned why the Indians were hunting so near Stafford Green. The next morning one of the young chiefs brought word that Opechancanough, the head chief, was ready to bring the yearly gift of a deer to the Governor, in accordance with the old treaty by which the Weyanokes yearly gave a stag in token of submission to the English Crown.

"Good," exclaimed Governor Spotswood. "Tell my brother Opechancanough that he and his gift will be most welcome when the shadows of the tulip trees first touch the chimneys of the great house."

There was to be a dance that evening, and by noon the coaches began to arrive, bringing the owners of the plantations for ten miles around; some came the smoother way, by water, in sail-boats or rowed by liveried Negro servants who sang at the oars. By two o'clock the music had begun in the ballroom, in a mingling of fiddles and flutes. It was to be an all-night dance, and most of the guests would not go home until the next afternoon.

Tamar moved sedately among the crowd and the Governor opened the ball with her as his partner in the first Virginia Reel. But she soon slipped away from the ballroom, as she must join Mrs. Macdonald in seeing that all the chambers were ready for any guests who might wish to rest for a few hours, and there were the refreshments to be supervised, and an eye must be kept on the servants' entertainment as well.

Tamar caught a glimpse of young Captain Dick Steptoe dancing with one of the five Denton girls, who were all toasts. Roger, passing by, whispered:

"Watch them, Tammy. At the last ball they danced for four hours together without leaving the floor."

Tamar laughed and hurried on. She found Mrs. Macdonald on her way to the kitchens, beyond which the grooms were lounging, chatting with any ladies' maids who were not busy decking their mistresses in the upper rooms. All was gayety and subdued laughter mingled with respectful greetings to Tamar. The coaches stood along the drive in the shade, their horses unspanned and taken into the stables. But on the box of one coach, Tamar's quick eye saw the coachman in Pecatone livery still seated. As she passed the man, she asked, "Why don't you join the others?"

The Negro made a gesture towards his ankle, which was fastened to the coach with a padlocked chain. "I ain't able to, Missy," he said simply. She glanced quickly at his face, filled with heavy pride.

"You run away?" she breathed unhappily.

"Yes, Missy," he answered.

There was nothing that Tamar could do, except hurry off to tell Agnes to take the man something to eat and drink. But her heart ached fiercely. Her father always said that well-treated servants would not run away. Why should they?—though he admitted that there were certain tribes among the Africans who were accustomed to be rulers in their own country and so took to slavery even less willingly than the others.

"But treat a slave with justice and understanding, and you'll have no trouble," her father said.

Going towards the kitchen end she met John Dummer, a heavy file in his hand. He greeted her somberly, for once with no smile.

"Where are you going, John Dummer?" she asked him.

"On God's business," he answered severely. "Thee is only a little girl, Tamar. Go about thy concerns."

"Don't be angry with me, John Dummer," Tamar said, taking his hand. "I was on my way to send Agnes to him, but I shall forget everything," and she passed on, with a lightened step.

She knew that she was conniving at what would be considered a serious offense against one of their guests —and she did not care!

About five in the afternoon, word spread that the Indians were coming, and the Governor came out on the steps to meet them, with a crowd of ladies and gentlemen in gala attire behind him. The music in the ballroom still played on, and towards this brilliant gathering of Colonial Virginia at its most gallant approached a small group of Indians against the background of the woods.

First came Opechancanough, a middle-aged man of much dignity of bearing. Over his shoulders was thrown one of the rare cloaks of woven wild-turkey feathers that gleamed darkly. His head was shaven on one side, and on the other the scalp-lock, tied with an eagle's feather, fell to his shoulder. Heavy rings of brass hung at his ears, and his breast was painted with red clay. As he passed Tamar she murmured, "Welcome, my uncle!" But, since his business was official, he made her no answer at the time. Behind him came eight young men carrying the dead stag on a litter, which they placed at Governor Spotswood's feet.

Opechancanough made a gesture of greeting.

"Father," he said, "I bring you once more a deer. Once there were many. Now there are few. My grandfather led twenty-four hundred warriors. Now a few score remain to me. Some have taken the path to the other side of the mountains where the hunting grounds are still ours; many more have taken the path to death. The white man's cattle graze above the

Behind him came eight young men.

bones of our fathers. You are our friend. Find a way for us. I have spoken."

Governor Spotswood made a gesture of welcome and acceptance.

"Brother," he said, "I have heard you. The sun moves from East to West. No one may stop the flowing of the river or the changes of time. I cannot give you back your hunting grounds. A new life lies before you. Send the sons of your chiefs to me, and I will put them as scholars at the college at Williamsburg. They shall learn the white man's ways. They shall be friends of our sons and teach your people all that the English know. Let us live together in peace. We will talk further around the council fire. I have spoken."

While servants carried away the deer to be barbecued over a pit already prepared for it, the Governor walked beside Opechancanough to the council fire that had been lighted near the James. Colonel Antony and a few other gentlemen came with them. The others lingered for a little while, watching the late afternoon light gilding the lawns where the pigeons strutted and cooed, and then returned to the ballroom, where the music still called them from the open windows. Tamar glanced along the line of coaches. No one seemed to have noticed that there was no coachman on the Pecatone coach. John Dummer had done his work, and she was glad. She hoped they would never find the runaway.

Afternoon darkened into evening. The candles throughout the house were lighted, flickering a little in the summer breeze. The ladies laughed and danced, or walked on the terraces, fanning themselves beside their partners, or strolled into the dining-room for cold meats and patties, spiced punch and cakes. The Governor and the other gentlemen returned, and at Colonel Antony's request Tamar joined the dancers again. She had been busy since dawn, but excitement kept her eyes bright. Her cheeks rarely showed color. They were a soft deep ivory, very clear and smooth against the dark sweep of her hair. She had an air of sedateness that went well with her face, and even in that room of lovely women more than one person noticed her and predicted that she would be a beauty and break many hearts in the years to come.

Dancing the Virginia Reel, she found herself facing her father and returned his smile. Just then, over his shoulder, she saw in one of the windows the face of an Indian, his black expressionless eyes fixed on hers. As he caught her glance, he made an unmistakable sign to her to follow and instantly was blotted into the darkness.

Tamar caught her breath.

"What is it, my love?" asked her father, bowing deeply as she swept him a low curtsey.

"I think I am tired, sir," said Tamar. It was not that she was secretive, but as yet she had nothing to tell. She must find out first what the Indian wished of her.

As she danced, she tried to think clearly, but the music kept coming between her and her thoughts. She had seen very little of her mother's people, who ordinarily lived fifty miles or more up the river. She had never been in an Indian encampment, but she had met her Uncle Opechancanough two or three times when he came to Stafford Green to consult with her father. He had on these occasions seemed to pay little attention to her. Why should he send for her now?

The music stopped—the dancers applauded. Tamar sought her father.

"Goodnight, sir," she said to him, lifting up her face to be kissed.

"Goodnight, little Tamar. Sleep well," he said gently.

But Tamar did not go up the great stair. Instead she walked quietly out into the darkness. The music and dancing had begun again. She looked wistfully at the lighted windows. Then, feeling very tired and a little frightened, she turned resolutely away, and lifting her wide skirts above the dew-wet grass, ran through the darkness towards the encampment.

VII

THE WAGER

COLONEL ANTONY went to bed at four that morning, and fell asleep to the sound of fiddling. It seemed to him that scarcely a moment had gone by when he felt a tugging at his bedclothes and woke to the sound of a small urgent voice exclaiming "Father! Father!"

As his eyes opened unwillingly he saw Tamar climb on the steps beside his high bed and scramble up beside him.

"Egad, Tamar!" he exclaimed testily, "why aren't you in bed, my dear?"

"I've been talking with my uncle," she said. "It was a council fire, a little one. Now I bring you the word."

"Can't it wait until I've had my sleep?"

Tamar considered the question. "It could, sir," she said seriously, "but inside me it wants to be spoken."

Colonel Antony adjusted his frilled bolsters with a sigh and sat up facing his daughter. Wide awake at last, he saw by the pale dawn light that her face was white with fatigue above a ball gown stained with dew.

"Tamar," he said, "you are too young to be running the woods by night. Your place is under my roof until you leave it for your husband's."

"I was with my uncle, sir," she answered, her eyes looking deep into his. Colonel Antony slowly nodded. He had never attempted to belittle her mother's people. Now he admitted that the Indians had certain rights in her, in which he would not interfere.

"What word do you bring me, child?" he asked quietly.

Tamar settled herself, keeping her back straight, for all her tiredness. She spoke distinctly, trying to think clearly.

"Opechancanough sent for me because there were many among his people who wished his lips to be sealed, and whose ears were listening when he spoke with Governor Spotswood and with you yesterday. My uncle says that the people of the French King

76

have followed the lakes far to the North and are building forts on the great river in the West. They speak evil of the English, arousing the Indians against us. A wall is being built and no man hears the blows of the axes. Many of his people are angry because of the ruining of their hunting grounds, and therefore would give us no warning. But you are his brother and he sends you this message."

Unconsciously, as she spoke, Tamar's voice took on the Indian tones, and the form of speech about the council fire. Her face was expressionless but her eyes burned brightly and when she had finished she made a gesture above the thick folds of her ball dress and said, "I have spoken."

Colonel Antony looked at her outlined on the embroidered curtains of his bed and thought how much like her mother, Shadow-of-Trees, she was at that moment.

"I have heard," he answered her ceremonially; and then continued in his ordinary voice, "What you have said is very important, Tamar, and to-morrow, I mean later in the day, you must tell the Governor all you have told me."

Tamar seemed to wake from a trance. She, too, spoke in her everyday voice, her eyes no longer seeing visions of small flames leaping before them against the darkness.

"You must tell him, sir. He will listen much more to you than to a little girl," she said.

"Egad, you're right, Tammy. You should have been a statesman."

Tamar knelt forward to be kissed, and slid off the bed, avoiding the wig-stand, her feet trailing as she went towards the door. In five minutes she was asleep on her pillows of wild-goose down.

"I don't want tame goose feathers for Powhatan's bed," she had told Mrs. Macdonald. "The wild geese fly so far! They will bring dreams of all sorts of things."

But that day, after the visit to the encampment, she had no dreams of any sort. Agnes sat on the floor by her closed door, a dark faithful figure that drove everyone away, until her mistress finished her sleep.

It was late afternoon before Tamar, looking refreshed, walked down the broad stairs. The music was silent, the last guest gone. She had a glimpse of the

Governor's handsome head bent over a map which her father had spread on the dining-room table, and heard one of the gentlemen leaning over his shoulder say, "Beyond the mountains, sir, we know nothing of the land."

Hunting for Roger, she passed by the weaver's house, and John Dummer at sight of her came to the door.

"Tamar," he said, "perhaps I was harsh with thee yesterday, for my heart was sore with the thought of what man does to man. I will not ask thee to forgive me, for we ask only our Maker for forgiveness, but I will say that I am sorry."

Tamar took one of his big bony hands in both hers.

"I think I saw him last night, John Dummer," she whispered. "One of the canoes went up river after dark, and there was a man with them who did not seem to wear his blanket like an Indian. I did not say anything to Father about it, since he might feel it was his duty to tell the Pecatone people; I am sure he would rather know nothing of the matter. Was there a terrible to-do?"

John Dummer grinned suddenly like a mischievous schoolboy.

"There was a fat body like a frog in fine clothes, and he was in a great taking. He even searched the weavers' house," he said; "but I just went on weaving and thought of the glory of God."

Tamar could not help laughing at the picture of the master of Pecatone. "Hush, John Dummer," she whispered. "He would have you thrown into jail if he knew, and even Father could do little to help you," and with a warning nod of her head she ran off hunting for Roger.

In the stable door she saw young Caesar and knew his master must be near. Sure enough, Roger was in Rambler's stall, examining his horse.

"Tammy!" he cried eagerly when he saw her, "have you heard the news? We are all going on an expedition across the mountains into unknown territory. The Governor says it will be like the knights of old riding out on a quest. Rambler is fit as a fiddle-string. I can scarcely abide waiting for to-morrow."

"I'll ride Kitty Fisher," said Tamar in equal excitement.

"You!" exclaimed her brother. "You're not going. You're only a girl."

"But it was I—" She checked herself. No, she had told her father that word of the French encroachments must not come from her. "You said 'we all,' Roger!" she wailed.

"I meant all the gentlemen with the Governor—not girls," explained Roger loftily.

"Well, I *will* go!" cried Tamar stamping her foot. She would show Roger she was his equal in adventure. Girl or no girl, she could ride as well as he, and outlast him on foot. He pretended he was her superior because she was part Indian, because she was younger, because she was a girl.

"I *will* go!" she repeated in one of her unusual flares of anger.

"I'll wager you won't!" said Roger coolly.

"I'll wager I will," cried Tamar.

"What will you wager, little Miss Spitfire?" asked Roger smiling.

"I'll wager the queen's crown against Rambler," said Tamar.

Roger looked more serious. Rambler was the apple

of his eye, and he knew that Tamar valued the Indian crown more than anything she possessed.

"I don't want your old crown," he said a little surlily.

" 'Fraid-cat, 'fraid-cat! You're afraid you'll lose," cried Tamar, looking disdainful.

"I am not afraid!" flashed Roger

"You are too."

"I am not."

"You are—"

"I am not—"

"Then why won't you take my wager?"

"Who said I wouldn't?"

"You did."

"I didn't."

"Well, you said you didn't want my crown—"

"I don't want it but I'll lay the wager just the same."

"Shake hands on it."

"You'll be sorry, Miss Tamar, when you lose."

"You'll never know it, if I am."

Tamar stretched out her small brave hand, and Roger clasped it. Already he was ashamed of himself for somehow beginning the business. He would give her back the crown, he thought, but just now he would say nothing.

The possibility that Tamar might win never seriously occurred to him.

VIII

BOOTS AND SADDLES

THE leaves hung listlessly on the trees, the English flowers drooped and withered, and even the birds sat almost silent with open beaks, and their wings spread away from their small hot feathered bodies. It seemed as though there never had been a breeze, and never would be again, and the gentlemen mopped their foreheads with their large lace-trimmed kerchiefs.

The next morning dawned hot and windless.

"Egad," said Colonel Antony, "it will be grand to breathe cool mountain air. We may discover the sources of the Mississippi, sir."

Stafford Green was alive with preparations. Mules were packed with supplies and camping equipment; from the cellars came small barrels, as well as bottles in hampers, of Virginia wine, burgundy, claret, champagne, and punch; the body servants appeared with their masters' baggage; the gentlemen adventurers were as gay as schoolboys off on a holiday.

"No need to carry meat!" they cried. "We shall have roasted game all the way, and berries for the picking, and wild honey for our journey-cake."

Tamar, in a dimity dress and cap, watched everything, her eyes big with interest. Early in the morning she had asked her father in Roger's presence for permission to accompany them, and at his refusal had retired behind a large lawn handkerchief, in what Roger might have thought an unusual display of weeping if he had had time to think about it at all. Mr. Bridge, going by, gave her one of his malicious smiles.

"In London, Miss," he remarked, "a young lady never seeks to compete with the gentlemen."

Tamar peeped at him above her handkerchief and curtseyed. "In Virginia, sir," she murmured politely between sobs, "the gentlemen need not be afraid of competition."

Mr. Bridge gave her a sudden stare. Was a Virginian poking fun at the English? He looked about for an answer, found none, took a pinch of snuff, gave a loud "hum," and departed to bully his servant.

Tamar disappeared once more behind her handkerchief, and did not emerge for half an hour.

By eleven o'clock, all was ready. Word had been sent to Opechancanough asking him to have four guides at Lilac Banks, where the party was to stop for the night. The Governor was dressed in a green velvet riding suit with high boots of soft Russian leather.

He swung into the saddle and waved his great plumed hat. "Gentlemen," he cried gayly, "on to the discovery of unknown Virginia! Let us swear to cross the mountains!"

The gentlemen swung their hats and cheered loudly, crying, "We swear to cross the mountains!" while the horses danced and the mules drew back their ears.

Governor Spotswood's keen merry eye turned to Tamar standing at the top of the steps, and then to Mr. Reid who stood dejectedly beside her.

"Mr. Reid! Mr. Reid!" he exclaimed with his unfailing kindness. "We cannot leave you behind. How

Governor Spotswood's eye turned to Tamar.

can you finish your ode to Virginia if you know only our lands of tobacco and tide water? We must have you as poet laureate of the expedition. Colonel Stafford, sir, may we not bring Mr. Reid with us, if Miss Tamar is in safe hands? On my life, sir, she needs no lessons to be the wisest, sweetest child in Virginia."

Tamar dropped a low curtsey. She heard Mr. Reid take a deep breath and looked anxiously at her father, who pulled at his lip uncertainly for a moment. Then his face cleared.

"As you wish, sir," he said, bowing. "These are quiet times, and I trust Mrs. Macdonald and the overseers completely. By all means let Mr. Reid be of the party."

The young Scotchman's rugged face lighted with happiness, and his gray eyes shone.

"Sir," he bowed to the Governor, "and Colonel Stafford, sir," with another bow, "I'm obliged to you from my heart," and he turned and ran awkwardly but swiftly towards the schoolhouse to put on riding clothes.

"Saddle Kitty Fisher for Mr. Reid," called Colonel

Antony to one of the grooms, "and let him ride after us."

A trumpet sounded to horse, the gentlemen cheered, the pigeons flew up startled from the lawn.

"But, Governor Spotswood," called Tamar's clear voice suddenly, "haven't you forgotten the horse-shoes?"

Everyone pulled in his horse again.

"Egad, Governor, Tamar's right!" said her father. "On these sandy roads the horses need no shoes, but we've sworn to climb the mountains, you know."

The Governor burst into one of his jolly laughs. "An old campaigner!" he exclaimed, "and caught napping at that!" He swung to the ground and his servant caught his horse's bridle. "Miss Tamar, how do you know so much? Tell me that!" he demanded, climbing the steps.

"My Indian uncle told me," she said. "You will follow the rivers up over rock, rock, rock, with the red pines and the vines swinging between them and the wild turkeys drumming and the sound of falling waters always in your ears. The stones cut through the moccasins like knives, he says."

All the gentlemen were crowding about while the servants led the horses towards the smithy that stood next the stables. Their holiday humor was unchecked by the delay, except for Mr. Bridge who remarked to no one in particular, "An ill-planned expedition comes to little in the end."

"Ah, but no expedition is ill-planned, Mr. Bridge, that gives us another one of Colonel Stafford's good dinners, as well as horseshoes," said the Governor. "How does the nursery rhyme go that my nurse used to say to me, Miss Tamar? Do Virginia babes learn it? 'For want of a nail the shoe was lost. For want of a shoe the horse was lost. For want of a horse the rider was lost. For want of the rider the battle was lost. For want of the battle the kingdom was lost. And all for the want of a horseshoe nail!' Well, now, we shall have the horseshoe nails, and who knows we may not win the battle, Mr. Bridge?" The last question came with a hint of sternness, and the secretary bowed in silence.

Roger was whispering to Tamar. "They say he jested at Blenheim when he was wounded, as though he were playing at quoits while the shells burst all about him. He is the bravest man in the world, I think."

"No braver than our father," whispered Tamar back, "and no braver than my uncle Opechancanough, either."

Towards evening the horses were shod and the expedition once more ready to start, for Lilac Banks was only ten miles away. Some of the servants carried pine-knots with them that might be lighted if the party were overtaken by darkness. The redbirds called from the oaks and catalpas along the drive; a woodpecker stopped his pecking on the great plates of a red pine tree to watch the procession of gentlemen go by. The late light turned the river to liquid copper and a passing sail to rose. Even the leaves and grasses shone green overlaid with gold, and the brightness gleamed along the whole cavalcade. Only the old hedge of arborvitae burned a deep melancholy green, setting off all the gayety that passed by it.

Roger drew back Rambler for a moment to say a last word to Tamar standing on the steps.

"Don't worry, Tammy," he said. "I won't take your crown."

"You shall have it," she answered sturdily, "if you win it," and waved to him as he rode off with a shrug.

The servants had stopped their cheering, and the shouts of the drivers of the packmules had died away. A dust like gold-dust hung between the sunset-brightened tree-trunks. From far away came the sound of the Governor's voice singing:

> "Come live with me and be my love
> And we will all the pleasures prove.
> We'll chase the antelope over the plain,
> The tiger's cub we'll bind with a chain—"

Tamar, alone on the steps, held her breath to catch the last of the song that seemed the voice of the beauty of that evening.

> "And the gay gazelle with the silvery feet
> I'll give thee for—

(fainter and fainter came the singing)

> "—a playmate sweet."

IX

RACCOON FOLLOWS THE TRAIL

TAMAR ate her solitary supper and sent Agnes back to the house-servants' quarters. With a pounding heart she wrote a letter and addressed it to Mrs. Macdonald, sanding the ink with a careful hand in spite of her excitement. Then she put on her oldest dress and tiptoed down the stairs. She heard Scipio moving in the dining-room and waited until his back was turned before she passed the wide door on noiseless feet. Keeping in the shadow of the trees she started towards the river down which the moon was making a silver road, but a few yards from the great house she hesitated and turned back. Running swiftly, she rounded the wing and, moving quietly outside kitchens and bake-rooms, came to the weavers' house, where a candle was lighted.

"John Dummer," she said in a low voice from the door. "Are you there, John Dummer?"

He stirred and answered her.

"Take care of the cosset lamb while I am gone, John Dummer," she said and was off before he could speak again.

The Indians were breaking up their encampment, stowing their few belongings into the bows of two forty-foot canoes, putting out their fires, rolling up the woven mats of their lodges. All was silent commotion when one of the squaws, glancing up, saw a child staring at her from the shadow.

"How," she said.

The child spoke and moved nearer.

"Opechancanough," she said. "I would see Opechancanough."

The woman pointed him out where he stood by himself, staring towards river and moon as though unconscious of any of the preparations for departure going on about him.

Tamar had a sudden knowledge.

DAVIS BRANCH
YOLO COUNTY LIBRARY
315 EAST 14ᵀᴴ STREET
DAVIS, CA 95616

"I must be quiet as a stone or he will not do as I wish."

She slipped down to the river and bathed her hot hands in the cool water, laying her damp fingers across her eyes. Then she slowly approached her uncle, and when she spoke her voice was remote from all feeling.

"Greetings, my uncle," she said. "I have a favor I would ask of you."

He looked at her without change of expression.

"Greetings," he said. "What is the wish of my sister's daughter?"

"My father and brother have gone beyond the mountains with the Governor, and I wish to go with them, with my cousin and the other guides."

"This is a foolish wish," said Opechancanough. "You are a girl and half a pale-face. If your father had wished you to go, you should have gone on horseback with the others. That is all."

Tamar waited. She counted all the stars she could see between the moon and the river. In a voice as cool as lapping water she spoke again.

"The part of me that is white has been brought up

all these years in the great house. I do not even speak the language of my mother's people. But in me sometimes the blood calls for the forest, for the dwellings by the spring under the trees, for the small fires that burn without smoke. For once, let me taste the life that my mother lived. I am strong. I can walk many miles without tiring. If I were dressed as an Indian boy, no one would notice me. My brother despises me because I am not all English. I have wagered with him the Weyanoke crown itself that I would go on this expedition."

"A foolish wager," said Opechancanough, staring away into the night. "See, a fish leaped!" He was silent, then added with the shadow of a smile, "I, too, have made foolish wagers in my youth." He seemed to think of the past, then roused.

"Your father makes too much of you," he said sternly, and Tamar's heart sank. "But—" She waited watching his impassive face touched with moonlight. "—The Weyanoke crown must not be lost to a head-strong boy."

The squaws who took Tamar in hand laughed and joked as they dressed her, and one held a pine-knot while the others boiled bark and deepened the brown of her face and chest and then painted them with red clay. When at last the squaws were through, it was an Indian boy who stood before them in leggings and deerskin shirt, dark eyes dancing with excitement.

Opechancanough grunted approval.

"Walk with straight feet," he said. "Place one foot before the other. Obey your cousin, Scarred Wolf, in everything. Keep a silent mouth. We will see how good an Indian you can make."

Tamar sat in the prow of one of the canoes, watching the dark low banks slip past them. Sometimes they went by plantations, and she smelled earth and the rank odor of tobacco plants as they passed the wharves and the far-off lights of a great house; but mostly the country was still scarcely touched by the presence of man and they passed only forests.

The trees near her were brightened by moonlight. She saw the glisten on holly leaves and ivy, and when an owl swooped past them, every feather lay in its place, pale and soft. The fish that leaped about them made widening rings of narrow brightness so that sometimes the canoes seemed to be passing through

Tamar sat in the prow of one of the canoes.

networks and spangles of silver; the path of the moon followed them up the river, and marked the wake that stretched behind them like the broad flanges of an arrow of which they formed the point.

On the far side of the river the trees were dark on a pallid sky and when, as sometimes happened, the other canoe came abreast of the one in which Tamar sat, lulled by the soft gurgle of water at the bow, the figures seemed to her to loom grave and dark against the light, more like spirits than human beings. Occasionally an Indian said a few words whose meaning she did not know; it did not trouble her. This was like her dreams, and she felt as though her heart had become a spring from which a dark quiet happiness was flowing into the night.

Nevertheless, after a time she fell asleep, to be wakened by a touch and a voice saying, "Come, little Raccoon."

The chill of the false dawn was in the air as Tamar followed the four young Indians up the slope of lawn towards Lilac Banks. She saw their lean sinewy figures outlined before her on a pale strawberry-stained sky. She might almost have been walking with four panthers—four panthers that were friendly to her and allowed her to share their hunting.

It was with alien eyes that she watched the great house awake, and saw the servants bring out the horses and the mules. The Governor rode over to speak to the guides, and she saluted him with grave calm.

"I have brought my young brother, the Raccoon, with me," said Scarred Wolf. "It is time he learned to follow trail."

The Governor tossed the boy a silver coin; the Raccoon caught it nimbly and slipped it into his belt, continuing to stare as Colonel Antony went by, and meeting for a calm second the glance of Roger. As young Caesar passed, however, the young Indian boy was bending over the fire, his back to the Negro. But young Caesar had many things to think of more important than Indians and Indian boys. Kitty Fisher had a saddle sore from a saddle blanket's having slipped; it had gone unnoticed by Mr. Reid, whose head was in the clouds, in heaven over the adventure. He came to the Indian campfire, drawn as a bee to clover by the presence of the savage and disinherited heirs of the land he loved. He even put his hand on the

Raccoon's shoulder, his blue eyes peering into a face which to him was filled with romantic interest.

"My brother is shy and speaks no English," said Scarred Wolf. "Now we must make ready for the trail."

Mr. Reid patted the Raccoon's shoulder and returned towards Lilac Banks thinking how much like Tamar the boy looked. "I suppose they may even be cousins," he thought. "Perhaps Indian children look alike. But his glance is prouder and colder than little Tamar's."

When the expedition set out, the guides led the way, on foot, in a swift stride, keeping ahead of the horses. Raccoon carried on his back a light burden laced with thongs. In the cool of the morning, the walking was an adventure. But they were still in low tidewater country and, as the sun grew hot and hotter and the dense trees cut off the breeze, the Raccoon dragged a little behind the others. At the resting place by a stream where the servants lit fires and prepared a luncheon on cloths spread with fruits and meats and biscuits and wine, the Indian boy flung himself on his back to rest.

Scarred Wolf taunted him.

"Is this the strength of which you boasted?" he asked. "You are a branch easily broken. Go fetch water."

When the boy came back to the guides he was given a handful of parched corn.

"They ride on horses and can afford to fill their bellies," said Scarred Wolf, "but we are on our feet. This is enough."

Once more the cavalcade was on its way, and now the boy was limping, so that the Governor noticed it and sent one of the servants forward with a horse. But the Raccoon shook his head.

"He was only dancing," remarked Scarred Wolf ironically, and after that by a great effort the Raccoon forced himself once more into the stride of the others. As the hours lengthened, the walking became easier and the agony in his feet seemed less.

That evening he fetched the water for the others without being told and found the sticks for their fire, laying them in a circle with their ends together, requiring little wood, as he had noticed Opechanca-nough's fire was made. Every muscle in his body ached, and he could scarcely swallow the venison which he was given.

"I was mad to dream I could do this," thought Tamar; but the other half of her which was the Raccoon gritted its teeth and thought, "I will"—and fell asleep watching the play of firelight on the undersides of beech leaves through which a few stars shone.

Scarred Wolf woke him in the morning with harsh words; but as the boy went about his tasks he noticed that someone during the night had sewn soles of heavier hide on his moccasins. He looked at his cousin, whose glance was expressionless. Somewhere the horn sounded to horse, and he heard the Governor's merry voice cry—

"Gentlemen, we are one day nearer the mountains!"

And, slinging his load on his back, little Raccoon broke into the swift Indian stride with the four guides at the head of the cavalcade.

X

IN THE UPLANDS

THE days went by, and the summer adventurers drew nearer and nearer to the mountains. The weather was hot and fine and the air of merriment with which the expedition had begun only deepened with the passing hours. The Governor was a man who could do serious business gayly. They would find out what sort of land lay beyond the mountains which the French were beginning to claim, but they would make a frolic of the adventure if they could. The long line of horses and mules moved leisurely enough. The gentlemen stopped to hunt deer and elk; they sang as they ate and drank beneath the trees. Sometimes they slept at the houses of planters; sometimes in their own tents. Roger grew into the beginnings of manhood, sharing the days with his father and the other men, and Mr. Reid rode with flapping elbows and knees, scarcely noticing his horse so intent was he on the birds that rose about them, the cornfields standing in full tassel, the snake fences, the hawks wheeling in the blue sky, and the forests of beech and oak, pine, walnut, and sassafras, hung with curtains and festoons of vines, and intersected by narrow game trails.

With every day the character of the country was changing, growing more rolling. Here, Mr. Reid noted, the forest was master, and the century-old truce between the woodland and the field which he had found at Stafford Green was here not yet begun. Instead of mansions, he saw cabins of logs stripped of their bark built in clearings where the stumps still stood ragged in the midst of the corn or served as barbaric fences for the thin cattle, their roots interlacing into a crude barrier. Here man was on sufferance. It was the wilderness that laid down the terms under which he might be allowed to live, a small mean creature, at its fringes. The courage of the men and women whom he saw in the clearings gave Mr. Reid a new admiration for the spirit of mankind; but it was of the wilderness he dreamed—the wilderness that stretched over hill and valley as far as his thought could pierce, still savage and untamed.

Two companies of rangers had joined the Governor, and in the evening Mr. Reid loved to sit by their fires and listen to their stories of adventure in the forests, planning new verses for his ode from the tales they told him.

He also came to sit with the Indians, who liked him; but the Raccoon was always quiet and aloof in his presence. The Scotchman seemed unable to break down the boy's shyness, though sometimes he caught the child staring at him with a friendly look, and once or twice he thought curiously enough that he caught a gleam of amusement in the boy's eyes.

Raccoon now could walk all day and swing into camp untired. He slept on the bare ground and drank water from his hands and ate sparingly of what he was given. Now he could speak in the Indian language, though with a haltingness that the whites never suspected.

Crouched over the fire, with the darkness like a blanket about his shoulders as he had always dreamed, he talked with his companions, who—now that he had proved himself—were no longer harsh.

"Scarred Wolf, tell me the story of the first Opechancanough, our ancestor," he begged.

Scarred Wolf enjoyed talking to new ears.

"He was a great fighter," he said, "bold as an elk in the fall and cunning as a weasel. He was Powhatan's brother and hated the English. In those days he led twenty-four hundred warriors. It was he who was the hand and mind behind the massacre of the whites that took place many, many moons ago, when he hoped to sweep the last of the pale-faces into the sea from which they came. His dream failed, though he grew to be an old man, so old that he could no longer follow the war trail; but even then he had himself carried on a litter by young braves and still led the fighting."

Raccoon stared off into the faintly stirring shadows. His blood was warrior's blood on both sides, and the first Opechancanough on his litter seemed as real and near as the Admiral Stafford in his flagship who had fought the Spanish.

In these days the Raccoon was learning to live very

close to the earth. He heard sounds that he had never heard before. Everything he saw and smelled meant something to him. By the behavior of the birds and squirrels, by the turn of the leaves, by the smallest breaking of a twig, he learned to read what was taking place unseen about him; though even then Scarred Wolf laughed at his ignorance.

"You have been wasting your life indoors and studying out of books made from paper," said the Indian. "That is dead wisdom. Are not the sky, and these trees, better teachers than Mr. Reid? It was from this red earth you were born, and your dust some day will blow on these winds. There is a spirit here that moves in the shadows, and cries out with the voice of the swans, and walks among the trees, and strikes with the arrows of lightning. Empty your heart of pride, and watch for not a grass-blade moves without a reason and that reason is important for you to learn."

At last there came a day when Scarred Wolf pointed silently from a hill-top and Raccoon had his first sight of the blue ridge of the mountains cutting the sky-line. To a child raised in the flat tidewater country it appeared very wonderful to see the land tilted thus against the clouds. The rivers had reached their falls now and narrowed to fresh-water streams in which the tides no longer ran; the road had narrowed, too, to a trail; and instead of coaches with Negro outriders they now met occasional packmen, with their lines of packhorses, trafficking on the wilderness trail, taking in cloth, sugar, rum, tools, and medicines to the scattered cabins, and bringing out the precious beaver-skins—tall morose-looking men in coonskin caps, with guns slung at their saddle-bows and eyes almost as learned in forest lore as Scarred Wolf's own. Governor Spotswood was as courteous to a woodsman as to a great land-owner, and more than once he stopped the pack-trains and invited the packmen to dine with him, giving them such food and drink as they had never tasted before, spread on damask cloths and served on fine china.

It was during one of these trail-side repasts that the rivalry between Rambler and Grenadier was brought to a head. The Governor had been questioning Sam Hutton, a well-known wilderness man, about what he knew of the country beyond the mountains, and after luncheon he had examined some of the fine beaver-pelts with which the packhorses were loaded, and in turn showed Sam Hutton the horses of his own expedition.

The packman ran an experienced eye over the animals.

"Nice young horse, that strawberry," he remarked, jerking a thumb towards Rambler. The Governor smiled.

"He belongs to young Stafford," he answered. "I should imagine that he is the best horse we have."

"Then you would be mistaken, sir," said his secretary quickly. "He's a good enough horse for one Virginia-bred, I admit, but my Grenadier would show him his place at any distance."

"It's possible, sir," said the Governor with an air of displeasure at the interruption, "but I myself have not such a preference for all things English."

Sam Hutton brought his big hands together in a clap.

"A race, gentlemen!" he exclaimed. "What better chance for a race? I'll bet on the Virginia colt, beaver-skins against tobacco at Mr. Byrd's trading house at the falls."

"I'll take you," said Mr. Bridge with an ugly smile.

"If there's to be a race, it must be to-morrow when the horses are rested," said the Governor. "And remember, Mr. Hutton, the laws about betting. We'll pitch camp here, and Mr. Hutton, you and your men must be our guests. Are you willing, Colonel Antony, that your son should race the colt?"

"Roger must answer for himself, sir," said Colonel Antony. "But I know he has long been an admirer of Mr. Bridge's Grenadier, so I believe he will be glad to show him some sport."

Roger bowed eagerly.

In a few minutes it was known throughout the camp that there was to be a race next day, and a hundred wagers were laid, openly among the gentlemen, and secretly among the rangers and servants. Even the Indians were interested, and the Raccoon was greatly excited by the news. A quarter-mile through a natural clearing was staked out in preparation, and everyone was airing his knowledge of horseflesh.

After supper the Raccoon felt a strong impulse to look at the two horses, but he was anxious that neither Roger nor young Caesar should see him, so he stood in the shadow of the trees watching the animals in the dusk. Suddenly his attention was caught by voices. A man's voice, which he recognized as Mr. Bridge's, was saying in low urgent tones:

"You will do as I tell you, George, or you'll have cause to regret it. There's no danger to you. Early in the morning before the grooms are up, take two or three strong horsehairs—"

Then the figures moved away, and Raccoon could see the English secretary leaning towards his Negro groom urging and explaining something; but what that something was, the Indian boy could not hear, though he followed quietly among the trees trying to come again within earshot.

When the others were all asleep, the Raccoon lay long pondering. Had the secretary only been talking of some charm to help his horse, some harmless superstition? But if so, why did George hang back? No, the Raccoon thought, there must be a danger to Rambler. He could not discuss it with Scarred Wolf, who knew much about deer but little about horses. And at last he fell into a deep sleep still uncertain what Mr. Bridge had meant by his curious words.

Then the figures moved away.

XI

THE HORSE RACE

It was broad daylight when the Raccoon woke. The Indians had gone so silently that no crackling twig had wakened him. He heard a hunting horn blow and a sound of cheering and knew that it was a signal for the beginning of the race. There was something wrong, he remembered, but he had not been able to guess it; and then, as he sprang up from the ground, the explanation came to him as clearly as though a voice had spoken, and he ran off towards the crowd in the clearing, running with all the swiftness he had learned in these last days.

The crowd was gathered—gentlemen, packmen, rangers, servants—looking small against the background of savage and indifferent trees behind them. The horses were already in place, but the Governor was talking with the riders. As the Raccoon ran, he saw Grenadier advance to another position a little farther along the course and knew that the black was being given a handicap because he carried the heavier rider. Raccoon's breath was coming in gasps. He saw Joseph Bentley raise a pistol towards the sky, and at that moment burst panting through the crowd and threw himself on his knees, on the ground, his quick brown fingers searching above Rambler's nearest hoof, while a volley of surprised exclamations sounded over his head.

"What's this? What's this?" cried Mr. Bentley in a sputter, lowering his pistol uncertainly.

"Give the lad a moment," said the Governor. "Let's see what he is doing."

Rambler, usually impatient of strangers, stood still as the Indian boy crouched beside him.

"What's the trouble?" asked Roger, leaning down from the saddle.

Mr. Bridge rode back scowling.

"Is this delay necessary, sir?" he asked the Governor. "Let someone give that boy a hiding for interrupting his betters."

Raccoon's breath was coming in gasps.

"Let him alone," said the Governor, who was watching the Indian boy with great interest.

Just as the Raccoon thought that he must be mistaken, his fingers, steady in spite of his nervousness, felt something infinitely narrow and strong fastened tightly above Rambler's left hind hock. Drawing his knife, he severed it, and rose to his feet holding three or four horsehairs that had been knotted above the hoof.

"Ha!" said the Governor. "I have heard of that trick for barely laming a horse. Boy, what do you know of this?"

Raccoon shook his head and tried to escape through the crowd. His one desire now was to get away from the eyes that were looking at him—Roger's and Colonel Antony's, Mr. Reid's and young Caesar's.

But as he turned, the lash of a riding crop came stinging across his face and another blow fell on his shoulder. Mr. Bridge had ridden up to him, and shouting angrily, "You put it there, yourself, you Indian dog!" was raining blows upon him. It was Mr. Reid who sprang from the crowd and caught the secretary's wrist in his big clumsy hand.

"For shame, sir!" he cried in a passion. "The boy speaks no English. He cannot defend himself."

Roger had jumped from Rambler and was running forward white with anger, when the Governor's cool tones cut through the storm.

"Gentlemen, gentlemen!" he said smoothly. "Stop where you are. Mr. Reid, release Mr. Bridge's wrist. He will not strike the boy again. Sir, I am accustomed to being obeyed when I speak.

"Now, gentlemen, we have witnessed the detection of a foul act such as no man of honor would be guilty of. We know that heavy bets were made on this race and must suppose this to be the work of some servant who was deeply interested. We all owe this Indian boy a debt of gratitude, but none more than Mr. Bridge who has been spared the embarrassment of being winner in an unfair race. Mr. Bridge and Roger Stafford, I desire you to shake each other's hands and the race will then be run."

Roger's face flushed and he hesitated as Mr. Bridge, still in the shadow, held out his hand, his teeth showing in a yellow smile.

"Gentlemen!" said the Governor again, and one

felt the force that usually lay hidden under his friendliness and merriment.

Unwillingly, Roger put his hand in the other
man's, bowed to the Governor, and swung into the
saddle in silence. He had not glanced at his father
for advice.

"Egad," thought the Colonel, well pleased, "my
son is growing into a man, it seems."

Roger sat in his saddle looking straight ahead of
him as Mr. Bridge rode past him to the starting point.
The pistol spoke and the two horses started forward
almost with one bound. For a hundred yards Grenadier held the lead, but Rambler was running as he had
never run before.

"Egad," said the Colonel out loud, "it's as though
he were as angry as Roger."

The boy's spirit seemed to have passed into the
horse—his stride was almost an onslaught, and as he
tore by Grenadier he reached sideways towards the
other horse with open mouth and only Roger's quick
jerk at the rein swept him past his rival and on to
the finishing line. There was great applause among
all the gathering.

"Virginia forever!" exclaimed the Governor, smiling.

But Roger listened to the congratulations all about him with an absent-minded look. His eyes glanced here and there, but did not find what they were seeking.

"Excuse me, sir," he said to the Governor. "I have an errand I must do."

"I guess what the young man's errand is," said Sam Hutton. "A pretty race, Governor Spotswood, and we wilderness men are mighty obliged to you for letting us see the English horse beaten. Not that fine things don't come out of England, like yourself, sir, and none finer, if you'll excuse the liberty, sir."

The Governor smiled and turned to Mr. Bridge who had ridden up. His eyes hardened at seeing Grenadier's sides bloodied by the spurs. The secretary was still riding with a heavy hand on the curb.

"Do not blame your horse, Mr. Bridge," said the Governor, still politely. "He is not accustomed yet to the land. If you will come to my tent, sir, at noon, I have important dispatches I will ask you to carry for me to the Burgesses. And as we are nearing the end of our expedition, it will be wiser if you will await our return at the Capital."

"I shall be only too glad, sir," said Mr. Bridge. "It will be a stride nearer London. And I am expecting word of a legacy which will make it necessary for me to return to my estates. To tell you the truth, sir, I shall not be sorry to leave this wilderness—" he made a gesture with his hands—"and—" he paused, smiled insolently, and added—"its varied inhabitants."

"Leave 'em as fast as you like," said Sam Hutton cheerfully, turning his back full on the secretary, and through a contemptuous silence Mr. Bridge rode away from the summer adventure.

But meantime, Roger had thrown his reins to young Caesar and, after a word or two of instructions to the boy as to the care of the horse and a pat on Rambler's arching neck, he was off towards the edge of the clearing.

He found the Raccoon sitting quietly, stitching sinew through a newly cut pair of moccasins, a red welt across his cheek. The other Indians were there also. Roger put his hand on the younger boy's shoulder.

"He doesn't speak my tongue," he said to Scarred Wolf, "but tell him my heart is grateful to him. I wish that I might take on me the blows that he received. Tell him I hope that some day I may be his friend when he needs one, as he this day has been mine."

Roger hesitated. He had a purse with a jingle of gold coins in it; but, looking into the eyes of the Indian boy, he had another impulse. There was a fine knife at his belt in a silver sheath, newly come from London on the *Merryweather*—a thing of which he was very fond and whose loss he would feel. He unbuckled it from his belt and laid it in Raccoon's hands.

"Tell him I give him my knife and hope that good fortune goes with it," he said. "Let it remind him of this day and of the debt I owe him."

The Indian boy still stared into his face. For a moment Roger thought he saw tears, but in an instant they were gone, if they had ever been there. The other boy said something in Indian, in a low grave voice.

"He says that he thanks you, and is glad of your friendship," translated Scarred Wolf, and eased in heart Roger turned back towards the tent he shared with his father. For some reason he thought of Tamar. Oh, better that she should be kin to the Raccoon than to some gentlemen he could name! He was ashamed to think that he had been ashamed of her blood.

Meantime, there was silence among the Indians. Raccoon had thrust the knife into his belt and gone on with his work on the moccasin.

After a while, Scarred Wolf laughed. "These white men are blind," he said. "His hand was on your shoulder, yet he never knew."

The boy said nothing, and there was another silence.

"Blind as a snake shedding its skin," said Scarred Wolf again. "But he will be a man yet, this brother of yours, whose friendship will be well worth having."

XII

THE GREAT VALLEY

STEEP and narrow climbed the trail, over bowlders, under the branches of dogwood, fording and refording the hurrying streams whose beds had made their pathway into the mountains. The horses, toiling upward in single file, stumbled and strained, some of the packs became wedged against rocks and were pulled off and their contents spilled, and some servants grew saddle-weary and were sent back. But still the pleasant summer weather held, and the gentlemen sang as they rode, or walked ahead of their horses, resting them; and still the Governor every morning cried, "Across the mountains, gentlemen!"; and still the Indians led the summer cavalcade, lean and alert. This was an Indian trail that their feet followed, over which for the first time rang the iron of horses' shoes.

"God bless your little sister, Roger," said the Governor, "for thinking of horseshoes, or we should have had every horse lame."

Sometimes the Indians allowed Raccoon to lead, and then as he climbed into the steep folds of the mountains with no human being between him and the unknown, his heart leaped with the adventure and inside his ears he heard the Governor's song repeating and repeating itself:

> *"We'll chase the antelope over the plain,*
> *The tiger's cub we'll bind with a chain,*
> *And the gay gazelle with the silvery feet*
> *I'll give thee for a playmate sweet."*

To a child born in the lowlands between the tidal rivers with the smell of brackish water always on the wind, and sea-fogs creeping inland among the tops of the pines and the shadows of sea-gulls passing and repassing over the English roses of the gardens, the rolling midlands above the falls had seemed strange enough, but these shadowy mountains seemed stranger still. The stream they followed Raccoon could leap across, and on every side rose cliffs hung with ferns, shutting in the view except for momentary far glimpses, vanished at the next step. There were many birds and animals that were new to him. One night a mountain lion screamed like a woman in fear and Raccoon leaped up to meet Scarred Wolf's laughing reassurance. The open spaces were full of brambles where in a few minutes he could fill a scoop of birchbark with blackberries cool to his fingertips. One dusk, when the birds seemed to fly in whirring haloes of light, Raccoon found a small black bear busy berrying too, and so unaccustomed to human beings was the little creature that it went on eating in one corner of the patch while the child picked in the other. For Raccoon these mountain days were full of magic.

But Scarred Wolf was anxious. Early in the morning Raccoon would find him standing, his eyes searching the horizon for the slightest wisp of smoke no larger than the thread of a spider's web; and late in the evening, he would steal away like a shadow, to lie on some overhanging rock, watching and listening for any sound that might show there were others besides themselves up on the mountains. But good fortune still smiled upon the expedition. Scarred Wolf found only the small ashes of old encampments, heard only the

The trail was narrow and faint.

stealthy pad of a wolf about the horses at night, saw
only an eagle gliding silently far overhead, examining
from his high flight the passing of the Governor and
his gay party.

On the third morning they seemed high among the
ridges, but the trail was steeper than ever and, with
the thick mountain undergrowth about them, it was
difficult to tell where they were. Raccoon was following behind the fourth Indian, walking in single file,
when Scarred Wolf called him.

"Walk before me," he said, and Raccoon obediently
slipped into the first place. The trail was narrow and
faint. It took all the wisdom that he had learned in
these last weeks to point out the way, but he moved
surely and lightly, aware of the faint hiss of leaves
brushed back by his passage, aware of the hoof-beats
of the scrambling horses behind him, aware of occasional voices. Suddenly he parted two branches and
stopped amazed. All unexpectedly, he had come to
the top of the ridge and now was looking down over
a far blue valley ringed with other ranges of mountains. The valley was open, a country of rolling grass-
lands, and in the distance Raccoon could see herds of

135

deer, and something of a shape he had never seen before.

"That is the valley of the Shenandoah," said Scarred Wolf's voice quietly behind him. "Few white eyes have ever beheld the sight."

"A rich hunting ground," said the Raccoon. "What are those others, not the deer?"

"They are buffalo," said Scarred Wolf. "The tribes burn over the woods before the leaves come so that the grass may spring up and the game grow fat. It is this that the people of the French King wish to claim. It is this that your governor has come to see."

Hoofs rang loudly behind them, and the Governor rode up. He, too, gazed long, then turned in his saddle and called back,

"Gentlemen, we have crossed the mountains!"

Scarred Wolf, standing beside him, made a wide gesture.

"It is a good land," he said in an even voice. "You are our father and mean well by your Indian children, my father says. See then that we are not driven from this land, also, and corn planted here that we may not eat, and white men's cattle given the grass where the game now feeds, the game which means life to us and to our children."

A deep sadness crossed the Governor's face.

"What a man may do, I will do," he said. "Could it not be, Scarred Wolf, that you too might plant the corn, and raise the cattle?"

"To you, your life; to us, ours," Scarred Wolf replied. "The gods taught our ancestors when they were made how they were to live, and this we do. Spread out your hand and shelter us."

The Governor sighed.

"I will not forget," he said.

The other gentlemen had ridden up amid exclamations, and now Scarred Wolf led the way to a rocky plateau that hung like an outlook over the fair valley below them. From this open place for the first time they could clearly see the peaks over which they had climbed, and the gentlemen, many of whom had been born and bred by the wide tidal rivers, uttered exclamations of delight. At a word from the Governor, the grinning servants opened a brace of wicker baskets and brought each gentleman a goblet of champagne.

The rangers had come up by this time and were formed at salute.

"Bring goblets for our guides," cried the Governor. "And now, gentlemen, I give you the King's health, God bless him!" The Governor drank down his glass, and at a toss of his hat the rangers fired a volley that echoed among the peaks like thunder.

"Burgundy!" shouted the Governor, and when new goblets were brought, he toasted the royal princess to another echoing volley.

Amid much laughter, the others of the royal family were pledged in claret, and then Colonel Antony called for rum punch and toasted the Governor amid more merriment and cheers.

"We must leave our mark," cried the Governor boyishly. "Gentlemen, the highest peak I hereby name Mount George for our gracious sovereign!"

"Then this is Mount Spotswood we have crossed over," said Colonel Antony laughing. "Let future generations remember the prowess of the Knights of— the Knights of—" he hesitated for a word.

"Of the Knights of the Horseshoe!" said the Governor. "For by horseshoes, sirs, have we succeeded in our quest. And now there is a dainty peak asking to be named. Who was the first to see this land, Scarred Wolf?"

Scarred Wolf smilingly gestured towards Raccoon.

"Young Caesar," said Roger, "bring Virginia wine grown at Stafford Green, and let us drink to Mount Raccoon." And he looked at the Indian boy with a friendly smile.

The moment had come. Raccoon had only to laugh, and say, "I'm mightily obliged, Roger," and there would be as pretty a comedy as anything in Master Shakespeare's plays. The wager had been won and need only to be claimed here on the mountain-top amid all the laughing gentlemen. But beside Raccoon stood Scarred Wolf, grave and dark, and beyond the motion and talk of the expedition a great quiet of clear air stretched about them, and Raccoon heard deep within himself a voice that seemed to say to him in the Indian tongue:

"Will your father be pleased? Will you not darken the sun for your brother? You have won—that is enough. Be content to seem to have failed."

So he only stood, a little bewildered among the eyes

turned upon him, and looked towards the Governor and then towards Roger, flushed and handsome in his saddle.

"Tell them both, Scarred Wolf, that I thank them," said the boy, and stood with a little thoughtful smile on his lips while his health was drunk and a volley fired for him, too. But no one except Scarred Wolf guessed that the small quiet figure standing there against the background of sunlit valley and far-off cloud-shadowed ranges was that of a victor who had renounced his victory.

XIII

THE GOLDEN HORSESHOE

TAMAR once more stood on the wide steps of Stafford Green in her fawn-colored damask dress with the string of pearls about her throat. She was thinner and browner than she had been six weeks before, and her dark eyes were even more serene. She knew the woods now, and the language of her mother's race. She need no longer dream vague dreams of them, lying on her pillow of wild-goose feathers. She had held the key to the forest in her hand, and now she laid it down again, looking about her at her father's great house with new pleasure.

At the foot of the steps stood Agnes with the cosset lamb. A light mist was falling from a gray sky. The guinea hens were creaking in the box hedges.

"I hear horses," said Tamar.

"I don't hear nothing, Missy," said Agnes, bending her head to listen.

Tamar smiled. Not long ago, she too might not have heard, but now she knew that sound to her inmost being.

"Father is cantering ahead," she said, "and there is Roger on Rambler."

"Landsake, Missy, you just imagine things," said Agnes admiringly.

Tamar held up her finger; even Agnes heard now, and the big cosset gave a sort of welcoming bleat as the two riders appeared at the gate. Tamar ran down the steps and out along the gravel, followed by the cosset. All in a moment her father had pulled in his horse, leaped to the ground, and gathered her in his arms.

"My dearest girl," he cried, tears in his eyes, "I have longed for the sight of you. Have you missed me, my love?"

Tamar gave him a great kiss instead of an answer. It was Roger's turn now to kiss her. "Oh, Tammy," he said, "Rambler *did* race Grenadier and won, too, thanks to an Indian boy called the Raccoon—a cousin of yours, Father says, but a little younger. We crossed the mountains, and Mr. Bridge has gone back to England. We call ourselves the Knights of the Horseshoe. Governor Spotswood means to claim the land behind the mountains. You would have liked the Raccoon, Tamar. When the Indians left us at Lilac Banks, Father asked him to visit us and he said he would."

Tamar's eyes danced. She had her secrets, but behind her hidden laughter was a surge of happiness. Somewhere on the expedition Roger had come to his growth—he no longer wondered what other people would think, or feared to be laughed at. Now he saw with his own eyes, and his glance rested on Tamar at last in unashamed affection. Unconsciously she exclaimed, "You're a man, Roger!"

"Well, you're a beauty, Tammy," he said, kissing her cheek again.

"Peace on earth!" exclaimed Colonel Antony. "Where have my quarreling children gone? Egad, it's all compliments and curtseys. But Tamar, my dear, here comes the Governor and you must save a little of your welcome for him."

"With all my heart, sir," said Tamar and, turning, swept the Governor a low curtsey. "Welcome home to Stafford Green, sir," she said demurely.

That evening the mist had ceased and there was music on the lawn while the gentlemen sat in their chairs and recalled their adventures.

"So ends the quest of the Knights of the Horseshoe," said the Governor, "and a merrier summer frolic I never had—" His tone sobered. "We have seen a rich kingdom, gentlemen. It must not be lost to Virginia."

A silence fell. Tamar sat contentedly on her father's knee. This too was her world, the world to which she had been brought up, and she loved it. She said shyly:

"I wagered with Roger, sir, that I should go with you. I wagered the Indian crown." She had either lost or won; she must not merely forget.

"And what did Roger wager?" asked the Governor, leaning back to stretch his silken legs comfortably.

"I wagered Rambler, sir," Roger's voice came from the half darkness. "But I don't want your crown, Tamar. Keep it."

She slipped from her father's knee and disappeared into the house. In a few moments she came back holding the crown in her hand. The gentlemen looked at it with interest.

"Here, Roger," she said simply, giving it to him. "It was my mother's, and her mother's before her. Value it for my sake, although you know they are not true jewels."

Her voice caught, but she instantly controlled it.

"My love," said her father deeply moved, "keep your crown. Roger shall have whatever he asks for in its place."

"A wager is a wager," said Tamar steadily.

"A wager is an ungodly and foolish thing," said a voice outside the ring, "and a lie is not fitting thee, Tamar Stafford."

"I have not lied, John Dummer," said Tamar turning towards the weaver who had been standing among the servants. The ugly face looked at her quietly.

"Thee has closed the mouths of Mrs. Macdonald and the others, but not mine, Tamar," he said. "I knew what thee meant to do the night thee left thy cosset in my care. Friend Stafford," he said, turning to Colonel Antony, "thy daughter fled from here the night of thy departure and returned here but last night."

A breathless silence fell. Tamar heard a moth striking its soft wings against a column behind her.

"Is this true, Tamar?" asked her father.

"Yes, Father," said Tamar forcing her eyes up to meet his.

"She was with thee all the time, of that I am certain," said the weaver. "She has won the wager, not lost it. But she is too tender-hearted to claim it." He could not keep the warm pride out of his voice.

Roger was staring at Tamar, his eyes widening and widening.

"*You* were the Raccoon!" he cried with sudden conviction. "That was why Rambler let you handle him. Why didn't I guess? Tammy, you are a wonder! No one ever had such a sister!"

"But I had told you you were not to go," said Colonel Antony a little uncertainly.

"A wager's a wager, sir," said the Governor. "Let me plead Miss Tamar's cause. You have the prettiest and bravest little lady in Virginia for a daughter, sir.

Mr. Reid, you must put in your ode how it was she who thought of horseshoes and then led us all into sight of the Promised Land."

"It was my fault for teasing her, sir," said Roger with an air of explaining everything.

The Colonel frowned fiercely, and everyone knew that his anger and surprise were over.

"This is not to happen again, Tamar," he said severely.

"No, sir," she whispered.

He reached over a strong pair of arms and put her back on his knee.

"Egad," said he, "put on your crown for you've fairly won it, and Rambler besides. Roger, you shall have the Belsize colt. He promises as well, if properly handled."

He went on, not noticing Tamar, who was silently shaking her head at Roger to show him that she would never take Rambler.

"You must," he shaped his mouth. "A wager's a wager." But she shook her head still.

The Colonel, deep in his own thoughts, began to chuckle.

"Egad, gentlemen, she had us properly fooled. There was I, her own father, and never the wiser."

"I knew it was Missy all the time," giggled young Caesar behind Roger, "but if Missy play Injun, Caesar ain't going to say nothing to nobody."

"A toast, a toast!" cried the Governor. "To the Knights of the Horseshoe and to Miss Tamar, their patron lady!"

The goblets were filled, the gentlemen sprang to their feet, the Colonel swung Tamar to his shoulder, and the garden resounded with shouts that set the ducks in the poultry-yard to quacking sleepily.

"I'm thinking it will take a good many lessons to put this junketing out of two young heads," said Mr. Reid dryly.

"Oh, we studied a great deal, Mr. Reid," protested Tamar. "Not in books, of course, John Dummer," she added hastily. "I meant the kind of things Scarred Wolf says are better."

"It's time for bed, Tamar," said the Colonel, giving her a kiss on her forehead. As she curtseyed before him, the Governor took her hand and raised it to his lips. He waited until she was gone before he spoke.

"Sir," he said to his host, "you have begotten the

"A toast, a toast!" cried the Governor.

living spirit of Virginia, the best that England and wild Nature together could make!"

*   *   *

At Christmas time, when the oak and beech leaves hung fawn-colored from their branches always faintly rustling, and the last great arrow of wild geese had flown south with a honking that set the dogs barking like an echo; when the Negroes hunted opossums on moonlight nights, and all the tobacco was dried and packed, and the last ear of corn had been husked; when Roger and Tamar had gone into the woods and brought back branches of holly and a Yule-log drawn by oxen with gilded horns; when the kitchens were filled with the smell of basting and baking, and there were no lessons, and John Dummer worked by candle-light on a piece of fine scarlet cloth that no one knew about; when the air was crisp and laughter came easily, and the cosset was larger than Diana, and Rambler neighed in his stall—in this best of seasons there came to each of the gentlemen who had taken part in the expedition a small packet from the royal Governor containing a little horseshoe of gold with the motto *Sic juvat transcendere montes* engraved upon it —"So swear we to cross the mountains!" Governor

151

Spotswood had ordered the horseshoes made in England, and each was addressed to a Knight of the Golden Horseshoe, who had drunk the King's health on the crest of Mount Spotswood.

There was one for Colonel Antony, and one for Roger as well, over whose beauty Tamar exclaimed.

"Wait," said Colonel Antony. "Egad, there's something more." He drew out a last small packet.

"*To Miss Tamar, the sole Lady of the Golden Horseshoe,*" read the inscription. Tamar opened the paper with careful fingers. Within lay a horseshoe like the others except that it was set with white pearls for nails and hung from a thin chain of gold.

"I shall wear it always and always," she whispered in delight. "Roger, I shall love it next to the dagger you gave me when I was the Raccoon!"

FAREWELL

Now in a waning summer, when birds are silent
    And crickets cry,
I finish this small tale of green adventure
    Of days gone by.
Farewell, dim woods where Pocahontas wandered
    And wild things dwell;
Farewell, you mellow lawns, and little Tamar—
    My dear—farewell!

Yale JAN 27 '69

DA 9/25/02
CS 6-24-10